LAND OF THE LIVING

LAND OF THE LIVING

Georgina Harding

BLOOMSBURY PUBLISHING
LONDON · OXFORD · NEW YORK · NEW DELHI · SYDNEY

BLOOMSBURY PUBLISHING
Bloomsbury Publishing Plc
50 Bedford Square, London, WC1B 3DP, UK

BLOOMSBURY, BLOOMSBURY PUBLISHING and the Diana logo
are trademarks of Bloomsbury Publishing Plc

First published in Great Britain 2018

A catalogue record for this book is available from the British Library

ISBN: HB: 978-1-4088-9624-2; TPB: 978-1-4088-9623-5; EBOOK: 978-1-4088-9626-6

2 4 6 8 10 9 7 5 3 1

Typeset by Integra Software Services Pvt. Ltd.
Printed and bound in Great Britain by CPI Group (UK) Ltd, Croydon CR0 4YY

To find out more about our authors and books visit www.bloomsbury.com and
sign up for our newsletters

The land of the living, sister,
Is neither here nor there.
We enter it and we leave it.
The dead in the land of the dead
Are the ones you'll be with longest.

Seamus Heaney
The Burial at Thebes

Perhaps it was only a leaf. Just one of those big hard tropical leaves gone dry and twisted and discoloured.

Something like that, caught on a dangling strand of moss or creeper in its falling.

A burst seedpod or a wilted flower.

Yet it looked deliberately placed, suspended from the branch of a tree that overhung the path, an ancient tree that seemed totemic in itself, situated as it was right on the crest of the ridge. It hung just above eye level where anyone who came by could not fail to see it, equally visible from either direction, sky behind it, the one open piece of sky there was amid all the dense cover of leaves.

Like a sign. Not chance.

That patch of light up ahead drew the eye like the end of a tunnel, and the thing at its centre, which wavered against the light so that detail and dimensionality were unclear.

He saw it first from low on the slope, looked up to it again and again as he climbed. The slope was steep so that he had to keep his eyes on the ground, on the rocks and roots, the deceptive heaps of leaves and slides of mud. He watched his feet, his boots falling heavily as his breath. He watched for insects, saw snakes in fallen stems, skirted thorny plants that threatened to close in across the path. Then once more he looked up to the light, and the little hand. That was what it looked like, the hand of a child.

He told himself that it was only his fear, that caused him to see horror in a dry leaf.

Almost, it is a hand.

But furry. And long-fingered, not child-stubby.

Not a child's hand but a monkey's paw.

It has been severed at the wrist, the hard bare pad of the palm stuck through with a bamboo spike, fingers splayed about the rough hemp string on which it is suspended, which is tied to the spike on either side of the flesh.

His own hand reaches out, tentatively as if to touch, but he doesn't touch. He only looks. He examines the monkey's hand and then his own, turning it slowly before him as if it might be some naturalist's specimen not connected to himself. His eyes pass from the one to the other. Fingers, thumb, mound of Venus, cupped palm; one palm spiked through, the other empty; each bearing its similar pattern of lines.

Not human. But some human has put it there.

It has been days since he has seen a man. He has seen monkeys, heard them more often than he has seen them, crashing through the foliage or chattering like a mob of children, so that sometimes he has thought there were children, waves of wicked monkey children playing in the trees above his head, laughing at him and screeching out their games – but he has neither seen nor heard any men. Three days it has been. Almost two of those days he has been on this path. He had first distinguished it where there was a kind of clearing, where the trees stood apart and there was clear ground beneath, and there was this apparent trail leading away between the mossy trunks and branches, narrow as an animal trail and yet it seemed to have an intention to it that suggested it was made by men, appearing to hold direction even as it wound back and forth, upwards or downwards, always upwards or downwards and never level, and some few hours ago – yes it was this day, he is sure, and not the one before – he saw in the mud the clear indentation of a man's bare foot, the heel holding water. Now here is this monkey's hand. No, not hand, paw.

Did that man come by here?

What sort of man was he, hunter, or warrior?

Dirt in the lines of the monkey's paw, a flaking rusty trail of blood. On his hand, engrained, the finer reddish dirt from the soil.

What is the difference, here in this place of war?

———

This is a place of war but where he has walked orchids flowered, high above him, pink and white and purple, bursts of colour rootless in the trees.

Shell bursts.

The flowers were like shells, Luke had said, bending his long back to pick up a fallen one from the ground. The form within was like the form within a shell.

So far it had fallen. Not jungle but ocean above. The trees submerged. He, they, in the dim depths looking up.

———

These last days and nights his companions have been only those in his mind: thoughts that connected and disconnected, that took on words and answered one another, question and response, to and fro. Sometimes he has spoken them aloud, but only to himself, and known it at the time even as he was speaking to someone other. Yet he has not been so far gone that he did not know that he must be silent if there was a man ahead.

Hush, he had said when he saw the footprint, the word a grey veil floating down on his breath. Hush, as he might have said it to the others, or as one or other of them might have said it, soft as telepathy, no need to speak or even whisper audibly as they all of them would have seen and thought the same thought.

There is a man ahead, some barefoot hunter, headhunter, hand-hunter, brown feet padding the path before them, and they must be silent. Or some other kind of hunter. Is it some Jap trick that now they remove their boots?

Once he had spoken they were with him again, the four of them walking the more silently through the jungle, watching the imme-diate path ahead, looking up to the trees fearing snipers or ambush, looking ahead and to the side and looking down, careful to look where each foot was placed, the man following placing his foot in the steps of the man in front, careful to brush no foliage, he pausing to hold back a frond with his rifle barrel for the man behind, walking with relief at the softness of mud or of sodden leaves on the ground, all his senses on the alert, even his skin alert, sensitised to the slightest sounds and to the smells that came to him from the trees and the undergrowth, wafting smells or smells disturbed by his movement, rank scents and heady perfumes of jungle plants.

The Japs must have come this way, or some pieces of this way, leaving occasional indications of their passage, opening a path, disappearing as the leaves and creepers closed behind them. Japs, one behind another, silent and single file, as they filed now.

On a path such as this one they would move only in single file, Walter leading, he at the rear. No point putting me up front, Walter would say, never gone farther than Norwich 'fore they brought me here. It was English woods that Walter knew. Spinneys and stands and breaks – and those planted only to make the pheasants fly. What Walter knew was open spaces. The flat. Stubble. Beet fields where birds found cover into the winter. It wasn't as if gamekeeping in Norfolk prepared a man for the jungle, but all the same they liked to have Walter lead. They trusted his sense of the wild more than their own, even when he led them into a thicket of thorny bamboo, the patrol lost then in a labyrinth of thorns, torn, silently cursing, unhooking vicious needles from clothes and from skin. You bugger, Walter, what do you think this is, a gooseberry patch? Tommy hissed ahead of him, the hiss carrying farther than was meant.

Hush, Tommy.

That word no more than a falling breath.

Where they came out from the bamboos, the vegetation became suddenly open. There was space between the trees for men to move apart, visibility high into the canopy, visibility at ground level in which men might see but also be seen. This must have been because of the altitude, that they had climbed so much higher. They stopped, took bearings, corrected their direction. Walked on, still climbing, spread now into a diamond formation, Walter at the point, he and Tommy the two flanks, Luke the runner at the rear, walking slowly, lightly, stepping like cats as they had been trained. Pausing at every few steps, eyes peeled, as trained, scanning arcs in every direction.

At any unidentifiable noise they held still, fingers to lips. That too was training. The answer to noise was silence. In silence things could be heard. In silence they became aware of every small sound down to the drip of moisture from leaf to leaf. They looked to each other, to each other's eyes, if they could see each other's eyes, signalled with their hands if they could not; and only when the noise had died away did they move on.

Tommy saw first. Tommy, always so quick. He whistled a single sharp bird-like note, pointed away down the slope to his right, to a narrow clearing where light shafted down. It was the site of a Jap camp, atrocity there plain for them to see, and yet they had to take their time, even though they could observe no life there but only death, and circle the clearing before they entered, climbing around and about it, cautious as hyenas about a lion kill.

How you could hate the crows

I'll make the fire, Charlie had said, leaving her in the kitchen, but he had gone instead to the hall and let himself out at the front. The dog had sensed his going, skittering behind him over the polished wood floor. Dogs are quick to sense when a man is going for a walk – but so was she, sensing the emptiness opening again about her in the house. He must have waited a moment at the door to let the dog through before he closed it. When he was gone Claire wiped her hands dry, that were wet and cold from scrubbing potatoes, and went to make the fire herself. From the sitting room she saw him walking out into the beginning of the dusk, loved in that moment his tall figure, a lone vertical moving across the flat, with that of the retriever – long-haired, feather-tailed – flowing gold beside him, the two of them passing smoothly out of the gate and down a track, beneath a tall hedgerow – that gold too, so late the leaves had lasted – towards a stand of Scots pine.

Khaki cloth ribboning to the ground. Lengths of khaki cloth holding men to trees. Turbans. Sikh soldiers tied by their turbans, their loosed black hair tangling in the folds.

They circled and all was still save for the flies. They entered the circle amid the buzzing of flies.

Untie.

Untangle.

Lay flat, line up upon the ground.

Bury.

He could not bear to look upon what was beneath their hands.

Dig.

The thunk of metal into wet earth.

―――

He walked a straight line out along the track through the field, turned a right angle at the end of it to follow the hedge. Straight lines. No tangle here. All straight lines. No sign of memory in this landscape apart from the square tower of the church which was all the distance he could see. No sound but the hollow thud of his boots and the occasional panting of the dog when she came to his side. He and the dog the only things moving, and a few birds spilling down towards the Glebe Wood.

The mist had seemed to come from everywhere, down the shafts from the canopy and up from the forest floor, between the leaves and the suspended creepers and the trunks of trees and the moss that dripped from their branches. The canopy was gone, the orchids gone, even the trees. Scents were gone, save for that of the mist in their nostrils and that of the soil which they broke with their spades.

The field was freshly ploughed, a sheen to the cold waves of upturned earth along the furrows. This mist here was no more than a faint layer, a fine ground-hugging English mist dissolving the surface of the land ahead. The dog ran on, then returned to him. They walked to the far end of the farm where there was grass and the herd had been out through the day. Though the cows had been brought in their smell hung over the pasture.

He had been walking a long time when the mithun came to him. He had slept out two nights alone, and woken and walked again for hours and seen no one. The mithun came through the cloud of the high jungle like a shadow, warm air blowing from her nostrils; smelling the human, thick cow-tongue licking the salt from his skin.

He heard her before he saw her, lumbering sounds on the soft leaf floor, snuffling, her dark form looming between mossed trees and hanging creepers. No threat to her, only size, her size and her slowness soothing as if she too should not be here in the misty tangle of the jungle but out in some green field, a big dark horned beast like a buffalo but gentle as a cow, she came to him, and her calf behind her, and looked to him with her dark eyes and put her black nose to his hand. Mithun were tame beasts. Where there were mithun, there should be a village close by, or a herdsman at least, walking with his animals deep into the jungle and away from the war. He looked. Waited. No one appeared. If there was a village he could not know in which direction it might be found.

That night again he slept out. He found a place where the roots of a vast tree stood in tall folds above the ground and there he made himself a kind of tent with his cape. It rained in the night and the sound of the rain on the cape seemed to him like massed men running.

Claire had the lights on inside the house; the two windows of the kitchen bright, a glimmer from the hall filtering through windows of other rooms. He turned back towards the rectangles of light. No need to go round and come back in at the front; she would know by now that he was out. His boots were muddy anyway, and so was the dog. When he got into the yard he could see into the kitchen and see her cooking supper, her figure moving first at one window and then the other, a slender dark-haired young woman in a blue-checked apron putting out some carrots to chop, a saucepan boiling on the Aga behind her. She had the wireless on. He could hear the thin radio voices that kept her company.

The dog pushed in past his legs.

You were out a long time. She smiled. Her smile was bright for him.

I went further than I meant to.

Isn't it pitch dark out there?

She crossed the room to draw the curtains and shut out the blackness. The dog curled in its place beneath the table at the end closest to the stove.

Won't be ready for a while. She went back and took up the pan and brought it to the sink, draining the water from it. She looked prettily flushed with the steam rising about her, loosening a curl of her hair.

Time for a drink. Do you want one?

In a minute, darling. Take them into the sitting room and I'll just get this in the oven first. I lit the fire.

Whisky for him, and water. For her, gin, ice, tonic.

She was mashing potato, then spreading the potato over a bed of mince, forking the surface.

There's half a lemon in the fridge.

Yes.

Of course, he cut it yesterday. Yesterday too he had come in and made their drinks like this, halving then quartering the lemon, the lemon stinging a small cut on his finger, he as detached from the action then as now.

The sitting room was dark when he entered it except for the glow of the fire. He drew the curtains and tended the fire then sat down in the armchair beside it with the whisky glass in his hand. The room only began to seem inhabited when the dog followed him in.

———

They had been sent to fight in a place of cloud. Sometimes the cloud was above them and other times it was below them as if the ground on which they stood was floating, as if they had come to an island and the cloud was the sea.

It was a place none of them had ever heard of and he did not think that the Japs would have heard of it either.

The cloud hardened and turned to rain. The lines of soldiers stalled. They put on their capes, even as they did so the column backing up behind and pressing them on. They marched on with the column looping down the mountain behind them, shining shrouded soldiers in monsoon rain. It was the kind of rain you might have imagined on a ship at sea, water the only element, hard spray against their faces, the wash of it at their feet.

They had come so far for this. A ship to India. Trains across India. Then this march up from plain into mountains. The Japs had had a worse journey of it, cutting their way through a thousand miles of jungle, but they would not know that until later when they began to follow where the Japs had fled. The road on which they marched was newly built for the purpose, rock freshly broken, surface laid, Meccano bridges the width of a tank thrown over rusty torrents thick with washed-away soil. Already the rains were washing away the new surface, sliding land upon it, spilling down the raw cuts in the mountains, erasing the Army's passage even as it was made. Heads down, they had stumbled up, turning bends, gaining height, walking into cloud, walking above cloud. And at last they had come to the pass and looked down on the cloud, and heard the sound of battle within it. There they stood to. The night was cold – and dry, that a rare thing – and they heard the battle intensify in the darkness, and they saw the flashes of it and slept only little, but in the dawn that followed there was a moment of stillness, and then they looked and saw the jagged mountains blue in every direction, and in this moment that was without fighting and without cloud they could see the vast bare arena of the battlefield, the smashed valleys and ridges and hilltops below; and even as they saw it, as the sun was rising and the yellow fading from the pale sky, there were the puffs of renewed artillery fire, the blasts carrying up to them in a separate time and unconnected, and slowly as they began the march down the clouds began to pour into the space again, strands of them slowly massing and spilling over the ridges and rolling out until all the view was gone.

The Englishman stood beneath a black umbrella and watched them come. Tall, long oval face, small greying moustache, stillness in his eyes. The Deputy Commissioner had chosen to remain with the soldiers all through the siege. Men said that he had been at the Somme. So all this must have been familiar to him. Who would have thought to see such a thing twice in his life?

Each morning of the siege, they said, the Deputy Commissioner had gone out from his bungalow, and even after, when the bungalow had been fought through, ruined, razed to the ground, and made the rounds of the trenches cut across what had been his tennis court and his lovely garden filled with exotic shrubs, and greeted them all, a straight-backed administrator in creased and muddied civvies; and if such a man was there, and if such courtesy continued, then surely the war would be won and the Empire would persist? He walked always with a Naga by his side, a wiry man of eccentric dignity wearing a red blanket and carrying a spear.

The Somme was bigger. This battleground occupied only a fraction of the area of the Somme, but it was a place of mountains, nothing like Flanders. No one man on the flat ground of the Somme saw the full scale of the horror. You had to be a pilot or a crow, dead maybe, to rise above and see the whole. Here even a living soldier might see the panorama, first from the distant pass then again, closer in, from one of the ridges, from the heights of the Naga Village. A soldier in the Naga Village might see what a crow would have seen of the Somme, and see the black birds also, the vultures and the big black Asian crows, above and below him, wheeling over the torn earth, the splintered trees, the craters, the smashed lines of trenches, diving to scavenge once the gunfire and the blasts had stilled.

———

You're sitting in the dark.

I was watching the fire.

Did you finish the Five Acre? She put on the lights. She had taken off her apron and smoothed her hair.

Yes, we got it done. I let the men go off home early. Wasn't worth starting anything else today.

I went for a walk this afternoon, she said. Down to the village.

Did you take Jess?

Of course, I wouldn't go for a walk without her.

But Jess was Charlie's dog. Jess had been Ralph's dog and now she was Charlie's. Claire took her for walks, out down the track to the village and the shop, to the post office today and to the churchyard and Ralph's grave, and Jess came with her, but soon as Charlie came in it was clear whose dog she was, lying now gazing at him as he gazed at the fire.

The silence opened up again. Claire's voice came light over the crack of a burning log.

I saw you ploughing. You had company. The gulls.

There must have been hundreds of gulls behind the plough, circling, landing, spreading like a white wake behind the furrows. These sights were still new to her. She had not lived properly in the country before she came to the farm.

Does one call them a flock? Does one speak of flocks of gulls?

Gulls don't act like a flock, he said. They're out for themselves.

She didn't know how you could hate the birds. How they had shot the crows for what they had seen them do.

When Charlie had nightmares she felt the sweat on him. She reached out, passed her hand down his slippery body. The smell of him was sharp in the bed. By morning when she had slept again it hung about the sheet and the hollow of his pillow. He had got up though it was still dark and there was no work to do, though it was dark and raining and he knew he would not be able to get on the land that day or perhaps for some days to follow. She heard him moving about in the kitchen and making tea, stoking up the Aga with coal – that a chore she was grateful he took to himself – and after a little while she would get up, and strip back the sheets to air the bed.

He was no longer a soldier when they married. She had thought to have walked out of the church as her friends had done in those other weddings that followed the war, with a man in uniform tall beside her, walking out beneath an arch of crossed swords held above their heads by comrades-in-arms. But Charlie was in mufti already, if a soldier inside, standing straight as a soldier, his arm beneath hers rigid as steel. There was the photo, in a silver frame on the chest of drawers by the window, he straight and handsome in his morning coat, she with her veil blowing across her. The wind had taken her by surprise as they came out of the church door, caught her veil and her dress. Because it was a winter wedding she had held only a tiny bouquet of gardenias. They were grown in some hothouse, waxy, perfumed, exotic. Charlie bent to the scent of them as he took her arm and she had wondered if it was a mistake and they reminded him of the jungle.

They had come here sooner than they had intended, hurried by Uncle Ralph's illness. There had been an urgency to make the move and take on the farm. Again, a wind, a kind of surprise, and they had found themselves here, full stop, the two of them at once living these fixed adult lives. But that was what one did, nowadays, wasn't it, now that the war was over and life lay so plain ahead? That was peace, wasn't it, what everyone wanted, the point of it all? One settled down and learnt to cook and started a family, and made the world a steady place. She lay in this bed, in this room which would be their room for years ahead. They had chosen this room though it had been the spare room before, since it would not have felt right to move into Ralph's. Ralph's room could be the spare one now, the other bedrooms one day children's rooms. Perhaps this was the better room anyway, at the centre of the formal front of the house with its view that already she knew so well, out over the flat fields to the south. Alone in the bed she listened to the sound of rain, on the roof and in the gutters and on the trees. This rain had come with the morning. It hadn't been raining when they woke in the night. Would the leaves go from the trees now, or would it take a wind to set them falling? There had been no wind this autumn which was why the leaves had stayed so long. Such a mild autumn it had been, people said when she met them in the village, the colours were especially pretty this year. There had been no wind, and no rain either, so Charlie had been out in the fields. Now with this rain he would be in the house. She felt the rain enclosing them both.

A mercy that it had been so mild, they said. The wind here could be bitter. Yes, she said, she knew that. She remembered that cold snap in the spring. Frost got the blossom, they said, that was why there weren't apples on the trees. Ah, of course, she hadn't thought of that, she was a city girl and thought apple trees had apples the same every year, rosy amongst their leaves. So new she was here, and no one saw that. There was a lot for her to learn. The wind here came off the North Sea, like the gulls. It came from the North Sea and the Arctic or the Urals. She did not expect that the gulls would be coming today. The fields would lie wet and brown and untouched, and the sky would not lift above them.

She wished now that there would be wind, even if this would mean the loss of the leaves.

He had made tea, put the pot warm at the side of the stove, sat down himself at the table.

Dismal day.

Well it's nearly November.

When do the clocks go back?

Next weekend, I think.

She poured herself a cup and looked about as if for escape.

I thought I'd go into Swaffham. Is there anything you need?

Early closing today.

Then I'd better go soon.

All the land grey through the windscreen, the road shining grey, the wipers insistent across the glass. The great wide market square almost empty in the rain. She parked, took up her basket, put up her umbrella as she got out of the car. She had forgotten what in particular it was that she had meant to buy. The rain didn't cease nor so much as lessen all the time that she spent in the town. The few shoppers about seemed blind hunched figures in raincoats or under umbrellas. The lights were on in the shops, a red glare to the meat in the butcher's window, a white sheen to the fish in the fishmonger's.

The town itself seemed laid out on a wet slab. She went past without buying, went on to the grocer's where the tins with their coloured labels were piled high in pyramids, tinned pineapple, sweetcorn, treacle, peas, Carnation milk, Ambrosia creamed rice. If she were to take a single tin from the base of each pyramid the whole shop would come clattering down about her, a shining gaudy earthquake of tins bouncing and crashing and piling, some of them stalling at her feet or rolling right across the floor to rest at the base of the counter. And she would stand still in the middle of it with her basket while the grocer in his long brown coat came running.

Just one tin of tomatoes, please, Mr King, she would say, And some lavatory paper. And a quarter pound of Cheddar.

Shangri-La

He didn't begin to tell her anything like a story until they were settled. Not even quite then. Not until they were settled in the house and the work outdoors was done – or almost done, done so far as it could be, for he was learning that the farm work was never finally done – until all those things were done and time had passed. He was aware that she was waiting. They were all waiting, the people who had been home through the war. He had seen that. They were waiting, and they pounced on information when it came out, as if they wanted to know it all. But they didn't really want that. They wanted the story but not the truth. That would be better for them. If they had only that, then they could put it in black and white, and lay it aside and call it history, and go back to their lives, and life could go on much as it had gone on before. The waters would close, and those who had come back, who knew the difficult things, would be only driftwood bobbing about on the surface. With time the water might seep into the wood, and make it sodden and heavy. With enough time it might begin to sink, to the mud at the bottom.

And then the water would be clear.

Claire, there was a Shangri-La. He could tell her this. This was a piece of the story that could be told, that she would be happy to be told, this piece that told how he survived.

He began to tell her at night in the dark, or when they went for a walk together on a Sunday afternoon. That was the best time to talk, when they were out on a walk, their eyes not on each other but on the fields, or on the dog as it ran ahead or snuffled in the grass, not touching but side by side so that they might almost touch, he inclining his head towards hers, stooping slightly since he was so much taller.

After I lost the others, when I was alone, I walked some days and came to a green valley. I saw it like a mirage, between the opening and the closing of the clouds.

———

When he looked up through the great tree he saw sky. For most of these days there had been no sky but only rain, and if not rain then cloud, which he told himself might itself be sky, he was at such altitude that he might be walking in the sky. But what he saw up there beyond the branches was distant, blue, beyond his touch. It drew his vision until he felt that he was falling away from his eyes.

He put out a hand to steady himself. The tree's trunk was vast, the bark hoary with moss and fern. If the boys had been here it would have taken two or three of them to reach around it. Not Walter. Walter would have been sitting between the roots having a smoke, taking his watchful rest, Walter always watchful even when he seemed most relaxed; it was his job, he used to say, it's when a man stops that he hears the twigs crack.

Look at this tree, Walter, how old it must be.

Walter missing Virginia tobacco, grimacing at the dung-taste of the Indian bidi. Aye, but likely it'll be holler, holler as a hatbox inside.

With age it was no longer a single trunk but a mass of multiple trunks and roots like elephant's legs, welded together to support and guy the great weight and height of the tree above. As his eyes moved up the trunk he noted scars like swollen lips where past branches had been torn away. Storms must have struck this tree hard, so high it had stood and for so long on the blade of this ridge, exposed above the rest of the jungle.

This tree must mark the horizon for miles. That would be why the paw was hung there, some territorial sign in it, though Walter might say it was just to scare the vermin. Or the poachers.

But Walter, from this tree one could see for miles.

Better be climbing it then, sir. (The way he said 'sir' it might have been 'lad', something paternal about Walter though he was hardly more than ten years older.) That is, if you're wanting to see where you are.

Looking at the scars he could see that when the tree was in its prime it would have been possible for a man to climb all the way to the canopy. Now it was so broken he could climb only as far as that first great overhanging branch, as the man must have done who strung up his trophy, the barefoot hunter who had come before.

No need to go further than that. That branch would be high enough.

He rested his rifle in a corner between two roots, removed his boots and laid them alongside. Scaling this broad first section of trunk was like climbing an almost perpendicular rock, finding grips in the crevices and folds, testing if the root ball of a fern could take his weight, at last hoisting himself up and astride the branch. It was broad enough to walk along. He imagined that the hunter would have done that, his bare brown feet light and sure, slightly splayed across the curvature, but he did not trust himself, not now, not in his current condition. The effort of the climb alone had left him dizzy. He rested awhile and collected himself, seated with his back to the trunk, then began to edge along, using his two hands to take his weight as he shifted his body forward. It was not so easy as it had seemed, because of the ferns and because of all the bamboo spikes stuck into the wood, spikes which must have been attached to other trophies long since removed or scavenged. So long this tree had stood here and men had passed beneath it, and men had done their killing and left their signs about the forest. He took himself out along the branch as far as the place where the thing was hung, from where the view was clear.

The jungle ahead fell away from the ridge as steeply as the way he had come. He saw how the dark crowded forest canopy dropped away into cloud, rising again from the cloud to another ridge and yet another, as, looking back, he saw the dark waves of it behind, the successions of hills and cloud and valleys in which for days he had been submerged. It seemed endless, this jungle and these hills, as if the blue line of the furthest ridge he could see, if he were to reach it, were only to be replaced by an infinity of ridges beyond. As he looked the cloud was moving, massing and breaking, skeins of it detaching and pulling away, rents appearing, skeins swirling back over the rents. He watched the moving cloud. And then for a moment as the cloud parted he glimpsed a break in the jungle on the opposing side of the valley: first an opalescence and then a glimpse of vivid green, a notion of order, that vanished as soon as he saw it.

He needed to be higher if he was to see lower, if the cloud was to part again. If he was to see right down into the valley.

Slowly, he raised himself to a standing position, pulling up first one foot and then the other until he was crouching, steadying himself with his hands, then straightening to find his balance on the branch, and as he did so the cloud at last broke apart and rolled up out of the valley altogether. He took this as a portent, the first sign of hope that he had seen in all these days. Beneath him, where seconds before there had been nothing but cloud, was an orderly landscape of rice terraces, greener than he could have imagined any green to be, tier upon tier of green terraces, neatly scalloped and composed about a shining ribbon of river.

———

He couldn't say how long the vision lasted. Only that the clouds spilled back heavier and darker than before and it was gone, but now looking across at the nearest ridge, where the jungle also had become darker and blacker with the change in the cloud and the approach of rain, he thought that he could make out what must be a village – no strange light on it, no mirage, but the plain straight lines of roofs amongst and above the dark jumble of trees, the only lines that were straight in all of this landscape, but so subtly defined that he would not have noticed if he had not seen the signs of cultivation first and had cause to look.

There was rain coming, Claire, more rain. The monsoon rain came in so suddenly up there, it was so sudden and so hard that the world could change in an instant. I think it must be one of the wettest places in the world, Claire, you can't imagine so much bloody rain, falling all at once, and it's so high there in the hills that often the rain turns to hail, with hailstones so heavy that people say they can kill an animal caught out in the open. This day there wasn't any great storm but it was torrential all the same, rain that made the way down slippery and blind, even within the forest, the water pouring down my cape, the path washing away ahead of me, so that I was sliding about blindly where the water went, unable to see more than a few yards ahead. I knew I wouldn't make the village by that night.

———

So long he had kept from telling. So much he might say, once he began to tell.

Time now in a farmer's winter. Land too wet to work. Days closing in. Their walk would end at four when it was already almost dusk. Then they go would in, and later there would be the fireside. The sort of silence in which men used to sharpen tools and whittle pieces of wood. And tell stories. Or women stitch. (Though Claire wasn't somehow the kind of girl he could picture doing that.)

Only the two of them. No world pressing in.

This was a regular walk that they would do. They opened a gate. Closed the gate. Walked on, along the edge of a field and through a narrow strip of woodland. A clay pit there, a deep dark little pond, and brambles about it. The dog disappeared into the wood. They waited, when they came out from the trees, as he whistled for the dog.

I did not even come to the fields at the base of the valley until just before sunset, when the rain cleared, as it does so often in the evening, and there was colour in the sky.

He wanted to be precise in his descriptions, so that she might begin to see this place that he had seen. Though the valley fields were already in shade and whoever had worked there in the day had left, he would tell her, the green of the rice still glowed in the dusk. (But how could it be so green, when the light was going, how was it that blades of rice held colour when the sun had gone? Was it only in memory that it was so green, so that what he would tell her now would not in fact be what he saw?)

I walked along the rims of the terraces, on down towards the river. The terraces were beautifully made, with walls of stone and copings of pressed mud strong enough to withstand even these monsoon rains, and channels between for the water to flow – this true, accurately observed, but he did not see it then, his attention then only on the ground beneath his feet, step by step along the slippery paths, along those narrow copings between and around the fields. All of this place was so surprisingly ordered and well maintained – this such a strange and surprising thing to him that first evening, so that he could not quite believe that it was a real place and not some dream into which he was descending – and here and there among the terraces were fruit trees – such a kind and pleasant thing, he would think in the days to come, that trees were planted prettily, for fruit but also for shade, where a worker might want to rest and look down at the soil and the crop and at the view and at the river gushing below – and there were big stones set upright in the ground, singly or sometimes in groups, territorial markers or memorials, or some kind of god-stones. In one place, beside just such a group of stones, in the bend of a tributary that went down to the river, there was a hut.

This was all he saw at the time. This all that mattered.

I found a hut where the village had its fields at the bottom of the valley. Just a rough kind of hut, a place for tools or for workers to rest in the heat of the day. More like a tent, with a rough thatched roof so low I couldn't stand up straight in it, but there was a wall of planks at the back that kept out the rain, and a kind of platform of logs raised above the wet earth floor, and pieces of bamboo matting on it and cloth, almost dry. It was cold but it was pretty much dry. It was the driest place I could have found. I was getting shaky, beginning to come down with fever. So I crawled in, and took off the rain cape, and spread out the scraps of cotton and matting, and slept.

It was the first night he had slept in any man-made structure since they had gone out on patrol, and as he lay there all the days and nights between, the terrifying nights in the jungle, merged and sank down within him. He shivered and listened, and slowly his body stilled. The sounds were different here. For the first night in all those nights he was not afraid to think that he must close his eyes in order to sleep. The sounds were the clear sounds that occurred in open space, the murmur of the stream close by, the roar of the river below. He slept and woke and slept, as the air chilled and a mist rose from the river, intensifying the cold.

He must have already been feverish when they found him. He could not take it in at first.

Daylight, he told her, and there was an old woman squatting a spear's distance away. An old woman laughing, prodding him with the tip of a spear. It was just a faint grey kind of daylight seeping in from the open end of the hut, but he could see that she was naked except for a strip of cloth tied about her hips, strings of beads about her neck and pieces of horn sticking out of her hair, and the strap of his gun across her shoulder. She was old, wrinkled, woman only by the leathery flaps of her breasts, and her black-toothed mouth was wide open with laughter. She prodded him once more and then sprang up, quick for her age, went out and shouted for others to come. She was spry and little and gristly, he said, so little that the gun reached to her knees. Then the others came, he said, and it was dark again.

They crowded across the opening and took all his light away. They were whooping and shouting. They were a blur of black heaving shapes. He tried to sit up and to speak, but the fever had made his head so heavy that he fell back again, and at that the blur whooped and shuddered some more.

Naked savages. In jungle stories the savages take the white man and boil him in a pot.

Claire stopped in her walk for a moment, turned to him, put her hand to his arm.

But, Charlie, weren't you afraid?

I don't think so, I think I was too ill to be afraid.

The crowd calmed and the old woman came back to him, and another old woman with her, two old witches squatting before him with elephant skin and sagging breasts, wide grins splitting their faces, and somehow he trusted them. The second witch put her hand up across his eyes and felt his forehead, and her hand felt cool and slow as a lizard on ice, and he believed that it understood as well as felt. She lifted his head and gave him something to drink from a gourd, then laying him down again she placed a cool cloth across his forehead and his eyes, murmuring as she did so, and there was a piney smell in the cloth that made him think of trees, not jungle but trees, lines and lines of tall straight trees. He heard it begin to rain, soft on the thatch like rain in a pine forest, and he slept again.

Around noon the first old woman came in, and two younger women with her, and they squatted in the entrance to eat from a basketwork tiffin, three generations of women successively wrinkled and bent, each wet as the other from the rain, but the youngest one had smooth skin and small taut breasts, and the rain made her slick as she moved against the light.

Wasn't it odd, darling, being surrounded by all those naked

women? Wasn't it just a little bit tantalising?

No, it wasn't at all odd. You just took them as they were. They wore their skin less self-consciously than clothes.

What he said was true in a way but there was a lie there also, the first of the little lies that he would tell her.

Even in that moment, through feverish and half-closed eyes, with behind her the shimmering screen of the rain falling across the entrance, he saw how the girl's stomach was long and smooth beneath the dark-tipped cones of her breasts and beneath her thick strings of necklaces – or at least he remembered it so. She gave him rice to eat from her fingers, and he took it feebly, and the rice was musky with the smell of her. Again he took a drink from the gourd, then she took her warmth and her scent away from him and once more he slept.

How long did he sleep? Was there medicine in the drink, some herb or potion brought by the witch, or was it only rice beer? He wanted to tell the story with precision here, to cover up the gaps. He could say only that he slept for an unspecified time, for minutes or hours, and that when he woke he felt a bit stronger. There was still that screen of rain across the entrance to the hut, and when at last he went to look out, the screen moved only as far away as the rims of the rice terraces where they fell to the river. No jungle, no hills beyond, but only these little scalloped fields and the people working across them weeding between the lines of rice, bent double beneath rain shields of woven bamboo that they wore tied across their backs.

They looked like so many beetles, he said. Working the fields bit by bit.

Beetles, inching through the green. Water pouring off the edges of their closed amber wings. He standing, shivering, before the hut. The fever in him, so he thought that in a blink they might open their wings and launch into rattling flight.

If they were naked, couldn't they just get wet?

She's playing, he thought. Not taking him seriously, not listening closely enough. For all that he had said, Claire still had no sense of the cold there. She assumed it was hot because it was the jungle, it was India. She was so sure of her preconceptions, of the Nagas and of him, of who she knew he was. And so she thought that the Nagas went naked because they were savages of course but also because people do not need clothes in the heat. She had not seen how a naked Naga could shiver. The rain there can be cold, he had to say again. This place is high and the mists are chilly and the rain too, so the bamboo shields, which stretch from the head to the hips, will keep their bodies warm as well as dry, holding their warmth about them as they work.

And some of them had little baskets tied to them for frogs, he said, and she laughed at this. To snatch up the frogs they found in the fields.

What for, she asked, to eat?

And he said, yes, but the French eat frogs too, don't they? And the French are quite civilised.

This was the way that it was easiest to tell her the story, to fill it with curious details, to describe appearances and customs, these people and what they wore and how they decorated themselves, their ornaments and hairstyles and tattoos – but these he had not noted yet, the tattoos faded on old skin, those of the first old women seeming to him no more than a smudging or bruising on their brown and wrinkled cheeks and arms and legs. Later and in sunlight he would observe all these things. He would see a girl held down by five women and writhing in pain, and the blood running as the tattooist smeared blue dye on her skin and stabbed a pattern into it with a long sharp thorn. The tattooist worked a broad band of pattern all round her upper leg, into the tender hollow at the back of her knee, the blood running through the blue of the dye. He will describe all that to her some other time.

My darling Claire, you have no idea how these women will suffer for beauty, he will say, you with your nail varnish and your powder and your rouge and your lipstick, you suffer no more pain than that of tweezers.

The men had tattoos as well. Many of the men had tattoos on their faces, dense blue mask-like patterns drawn across forehead and cheeks and about the mouth, and over their chests and limbs. The older the men, the grander but more blurred the designs. These tattoos also he would note. He did not know what they meant. He would not know that until he met Hussey who had spoken with anthropologists and studied every tribe that he encountered. It was better then that he did not know, or he would have been more afraid.

The beetles worked on, and it was a long time before the rain ceased. The stream rushed beside the hut, the river in its narrow gorge below. He could hear the sound of the waters beneath the rain. He knew the source of the sound and yet it seemed to come only from a swirling torrent within his head. When finally the Nagas finished work and took him with them up to the village, he would cross the river on a swaying bamboo bridge, feet in ungainly boots first one then the other over the brown dizzy blur, looking down because he had to, focusing on those feet that seemed clown's feet, out of proportion and almost detached from himself, feet that would become heavier, step by step, as he climbed all the way to that village he had seen on the ridge.

I haven't said, have I, why the Naga villages are all situated on ridges? It's because of the raids. The headhunting. It's true, you know. They do hunt heads. They always have.

Not really, not now, surely? Not any more?

Yes, some of them. Even now. So their villages are built on the high ridges, even if this means they have to walk down a thousand or two thousand feet to their fields, even if they have to go a long way for water. But they think nothing of it. They'd be surprised to see how people in England like to live in the valleys. Perhaps they'd be afraid to live in a valley, or in flat country like this where they could see no views. Those women there – most of the farm work is done by the women there – they walk down for an hour, an hour and a half, to begin work in the morning, and do hard physical labour all day, and walk back up in the evening, even the old ones, tough old birds, with baskets on their backs with crops in them, or fruit, or firewood. I was hard put to follow, so weak as I was. We skirted the terraces, and met other villagers coming in, other women and some men too, crazy, wild-looking fellows, most of them carrying daos with wicked-looking blades. They all got terribly excited to see me, laughing and chattering. Sometimes they got so excited with talking about me that they skittered on and didn't notice that they left me behind them walking alone. It didn't matter. There was nothing I could do but follow them. Nothing else I'd have thought of doing. The terraces came to an end in groves of bamboo and thin forest, but the path went up clear and straight. I couldn't be lost even though they'd gone on so fast ahead.

Where the mountain grew steeper, the path turned to steps. He could see the file of field workers high above him on the steps, a long stone staircase so well laid and mossed and lichened that it might have been built by some ancient civilisation.

It was as if I'd gone back centuries, Claire. There I was, struggling up from the terraces down below to the village above, and the people walked ahead of me the way they must have walked each day for centuries, all the way up and all the way down, these files of brown naked figures like slaves in an Egyptian painting – only they weren't slaves, they were a tribe, a community, and they seemed such a fine community when I got to know them, good-humoured and equal and happy.

Of course he was not thinking any of that at the time. At the time he was conscious only of the effort of the climb, the weight of his legs and the pounding inside his head. There were platforms set at intervals alongside the steps, and on one of these his particular women waited for him. They let him rest and then the strongest of them, the middle one, took up his pack and added it to the load in her basket, which she carried by a strap across her forehead, and he was too weak to refuse though he saw that her basket had weight in it already. Slowly, she went on, bent low and with the girl beside her, and he followed, and the old woman came behind, still wearing his gun and chivvying him with gruff single words such as at home one spoke to animals. As they climbed on, the sky cleared above so that he could begin to see the huts of the village spread along the crest of the ridge, a sheen of light on tobacco-coloured palm-leaf roofs.

Close beneath the village the path narrowed and ran between high stone walls. There was a stone gateway with a wooden door made from a single huge slab of wood.

It was this thick, he said, holding out his hand splayed with the palm towards her. The whole front of the door was carved, with a design of a skull and huge horns, painted like a mask in red and white and black, a scary mask to repel intruders – or perhaps it was more than that, perhaps it had magical power, I don't know – and two men waited at the door. I think that they were waiting for us, because when we had entered they swung the massive door shut and barred it for the night. Beyond the gate was a steep narrow passage, rising and turning between high walls – part of the defences, I suppose, like the passage at the entrance of a castle, that would have been hard to fight through, if any attacker had made it through the gate. Later I saw all this properly and understood its purpose, how the whole village was built like a fort. At the time I was just walking blindly, putting a hand to the wall for support, as we climbed more steps, steep, up and up, until we came out at the top of the ridge, at an open circular platform that looked out over the valley. There were men seated all round the edge of the platform, and the old woman led me into the centre of the circle. I stood there panting. Dazed as if I had been brought out from the dark. The men stayed squatting where they were and looked at me, the sky so bright behind them that I couldn't see their faces so much as their forms against it, bizarre outlines they made with their headgear of tusks and horns and fur and feathers. I wish you could imagine the moment, he said, picturing it to himself as he had not seen it then: this high place, a horizon all round of endlessly receding jungle ridges, the sun going down, one lost white man surrounded by a crowd of natives, they jabbering among themselves, arguing by the sound of it, currents of speech swirling across this way and that, utterly unintelligible.

Again she asked, but wasn't he afraid?

He told her that he was scarcely conscious enough for fear.

His mind was removed from himself, so that he knew sensation and not thought, knew only the sensations of that moment without before or after. Perhaps without sense of time there is no fear. Not even identity. He had seen that in battle, known it, known only the immediate moment. The absence of time and the absence of self. So now in this moment of which he spoke he stood reeling, and yes, he must have been aware somewhere in his consciousness that the great gate was barred behind him, that these men were headhunters and that he Charlie Ashe was the cause of the hubbub, but what was most in his mind, the memory that he had taken away and that came back to him, was nothing personal but only a sense of space, of endless wheeling space. He felt it even as he spoke to her, as if he was on a cliff high above and she was far and small below. Yet it wasn't the looking down that gave him vertigo but the looking up – the shock, after such a climb, of having nothing but sky above, and such a vast sky as this one. Vast, pale at this moment of sunset, clear to the first stars. When he looked down to earth again the figures of the men as they came and pressed in close seemed almost insignificant.

Say no more for a while. The dog walked quiet at their heels, knowing they were nearly home.

———

Darkness. Hands on him. Voices of women, not men. Women giggling. In the darkness, a flicker of light as of a candle flame – no, more light than that, the flames of a fire. A fire burned some yards away from him, the women moving between the place where he lay and the fire. There was no sky any more. He was in a hut and there was only the light of the fire, these women leaning over him as they untied the laces on his boots, clumsy as they didn't know where to pull, as they fumbled at the buttons on his shirt and his shorts. Hands lifted his back. They took his shirt off him, the cotton clinging where it was wet with sweat. He recognised the youngest of the women from the field. There were other faces besides hers, coming and going, he was not sure how many. One girl put out a bold hand and stroked the hairs of his chest. There was light enough to see that she was pretty, there was light on her cheeks and her eyes. She laughed, a light airy laugh, but her mouth was a black hole.

———

The women of that tribe paint their teeth black, you know, to be beautiful.

Sounds rather ugly to me. Claire's smile was the whiter for the red of her lipstick. She had taken off her headscarf and put her fingers through her hair as she went to fill a bowl of water for the dog.

Yes, well, it's disconcerting.

A doubt went through him. Was this where the story must always come to an end? Here in this farmhouse, against the sound of the dog drinking, muddy paw-prints across the kitchen floor. Because he had to tell it this way, didn't he? Because that was what a chap did, wasn't it, coming home, what chaps did who came home with this kind of story in them? Because he was Charlie, and that was the sort of person he was, at home, who made jokes and who made things matter-of-fact; the person she expected him to be, who must be matter-of-fact with her because she did not know that other man he might have been or might be inside. So pretty she was in this moment, just come indoors, looking fresh, laughing at what he said. She was filling the kettle, lifting the lid of the Aga, placing the kettle there to boil, a teapot to warm beside it.

When I first noticed the old women with black teeth I thought it was disease. Then I saw all the women had them. They make up some black jungle paste and smear it on.

Oh do they really? She spoke as if he was pulling her leg.

Smooth girls' faces, dark eyes, so many black mouths giggling to see such a pale and hairy man. An old warrior with a necklace of brass heads pushing the girls aside, taking up his wrist in his hand, looking him over. He made some comment that caused the girls to howl and crease up with laughter, but all the time kept hold of his arm as if he was sizing up the flesh on his bones.

Tell it straight, he told himself. Take this moment, when there is such ease between you. Sit and tell the rest, over the kitchen table. You don't have to meet her eyes. She doesn't sit for long anyway, but gets up and leaves her tea unfinished and moves about, opening the fridge, deciding what she will make for supper. You watch her move, her hands, the back of her as she ties her apron. Put your own hand flat to the surface of the table, to the crisp yellow cotton of the cloth, smooth to the touch. And speak.

They looked after me. I must have fainted up there, after the climb, and they took me into a hut and cared for me until I was better. I don't know how many days it was. At first I had a fever, then I was too weak to move. The hut was always dark. All the light in it came from the entrance, and from the fire they kept burning from morning to evening at the centre of the room. At that time of year in the rains there's so little daylight anyway, there wasn't so much difference, inside, between day and night. Their huts are big, long, barn-like, a single long room with sleeping areas partitioned off by screens of plaited bamboo. There's the fire in the middle, no chimney but the smoke rising up through the thatch of the roof, and everything is permeated and sooty-black with the smoke.

The smell of smoke would cling to his skin and to everything he had. When he left the village the smell would go with him, and it stayed when he had washed and his clothes had been washed many times. Even now at home it came back to him at times. He would smell it in the ash and the half-burnt logs on the hearth when the fire was dead, or more powerfully when the rain had wet the remains of a bonfire, because always there had been dampness beside the smoke, but sometimes it would come to him unexpectedly in the bright dry open air as if any chance thought of the place carried the scent.

———

They must have been debating what to do with me that moment when I first got up to the village. I think that was why the men had come together in the circle. Someone had brought up the news from the fields, and the chief had called a meeting. I never again saw so many warriors together there. Later, when I'd recovered enough to wander about, those weeks before I left, I'd go to the circle, if it wasn't raining, but I only ever met a handful of men up there at any one time.

I think they had already decided they would keep me until the rains ended and it was possible to travel. I think that it must have been a communal decision, though I lived with the family of the women who first found me.

Why, what for?

Just kindness, I suppose. Just, what people do.

And then he told her the simple things, how it was. How the family who took him in seemed to be quite an eminent family. They had a big hut with carved posts at the entrance, and wooden gable ends like horns standing out above the thatch.

I wish I had my sketches to show you. I tried to sketch it all later for Hussey, when I got to Hussey, the plan and style of the house, the carvings there and elsewhere in the village. I mapped out the village for him as well as I could. I had time to get to know the village well. It was spread along a smooth high shoulder of mountain with a cliff to one end of it and a steep, densely jungled peak to the other. The huts looked wonderfully shaggy with their palm-leaf thatch, perched wherever there was flat ground. Hussey says that the biggest huts are clan houses where the young men live and sleep. These have pillars with carvings, and huge log drums outside made out of whole tree trunks, and close to each of these huts there is always a circle like the one I first came to, constructed at some vantage point from which the men can watch for raiding parties from the surrounding valleys. These are all pretty much the same, levelled circles with stones a foot high set as seats around the edge, but that first one was the grandest, the sitting stones there carved like the village gate. I drew the design of the gate for Hussey, as well as I could remember it.

And I drew the weird things. I haven't told you about those, have I?

No, you haven't. Tell me the weird things. Claire paused in her cooking.

There was the head post. Close to that first circle, a grisly structure of poles hung with skulls, and around it a crowd of upright stones, menhirs as Hussey called them, that they put up to record headhunting raids.

Ugh, Charlie, human skulls?

Yes.

Not new ones surely?

I don't know. Just skulls.

Here and there through the village were these groups of stones, about which they do wild dances, Hussey says, when there is a festival or a celebration, or when there has been a raid and there are new heads to string from the post. And there were the clan houses, which had those horns above their roofs and carved posts to their porches, and, outside and inside, more hanging skulls, some of them whole, some of them just the front and the upper part of the face, with the lower jaw removed, because that's where the power in a head lies, in the front of the skull and the upper part, behind the eyes. According to what Hussey says, these halved skulls may have been brought from the most distant raids. When a raiding party has a long way to travel, they're much easier to carry like that.

Well I hadn't thought of that, Claire said, as she took out a knife from a drawer. Her voice was the crisp sort of voice she might have used to talk about a recipe or some little practical matter.

Of what?

Of how you carried skulls about.

Well, no, of course not. One wouldn't, would one?

He saw that it was rather an odd thing to be speaking of. There were things that were too odd in her world to be spoken. That became no more than distractions when you said them like this, as if they didn't matter.

She took the knife and she took a chopping board and placed them on the table. She went to the fridge to find in it whatever she meant to chop. He spoke to her back, to the curls in her hair, and her tidy waist about which he liked to put his hands, and the untidy apron string about it which he would have liked to untie.

All these things, he said, going on with the distractions, not saying what else he might have said but only the unnecessary things; these details, he said, were the sort of things Hussey wanted to know. You see, this was some place way out in the unadministered areas. Hussey had never been there. So far as he knew, no white man had ever set foot there before me. And I didn't even know its name, or the name of its people or the language they spoke. The drawings and descriptions I gave him meant that he thought he could identify the tribal grouping, but there were elements that were unique, that made him wonder if they might have been some other tribe as yet entirely unrecorded. All I could bring him was whatever I could think to remember and a guess at the direction in which the place lay, so many days' walk east of Mokokchung. I had tried to keep at least an approximate notion of its location. I had my compass after all.

Sometimes for days on end there was no view because of the cloud and the rain. He would walk the narrow paths between the tawny brooding huts and the moving strands of mist to one of the viewing platforms, and squat on a stool that was too low for the length of his legs, and look out into nothingness, and some of the children who always followed wherever he walked in the village would cluster a little way off and watch him as he looked. Some days the cloud was so dense across the ridge that he scarcely saw even the children. Other days it massed below in a sullen grey sea. Once when the sky was clear he saw aeroplanes in the far distance. They were so far off that he could not have said whether they were Japanese fighters come to attack the British or British ones gone after the Japanese, or American bombers on their way to China.

We make love when you've been talking about your village. Do you notice that?

That's only because it's Sunday and we went for a walk, and we talked when we were on the walk. His voice came lightly as he lay on his back beside her in bed.

And then? She lifted herself up on an elbow, face close to his. She wanted him to look at her.

And then we came in. And we had tea, and then you had a bath. And when you came out from the bath you were warm and clean. And naked, of course.

Like they were in the village.

But they weren't so clean.

I think you liked it there.

Yes, I told you, it was a Shangri-La.

But, darling, they were headhunters, not mystic Tibetans.

That's not the point.

Why didn't they let you go sooner?

Because of the rain at first. The rivers were all in spate. No one was going anywhere.

Didn't you ever feel a prisoner?

No, actually, I don't think I did. Except those days, and there could be days on end, when the rain wouldn't stop, and then I felt a prisoner of the rain.

Oh.

Sometimes I felt I was a castaway.

Then would you have made a fire? Signalled from the beach for some ship to come?

He turned away from her onto his side, to face the window. That would have been hard. It was so wet, everything was wet and covered in mould. There were mushrooms growing in my boots.

Darling, don't tease!

It's true. I didn't wear my boots for a while, and when I got to them again they were sprouting mushrooms.

She put her arm across him. You did like it there.

Yes, in a way. I did.

It had got dark while they were in bed.

We should draw the curtains.

She got up and stepped over his clothes on the floor and went to the window, pulling the curtains from the side just in case anyone was out there to see her. He hadn't moved so she got back into the bed beside him where it was warm. He didn't move then either, to welcome her back. He was still looking to where she had drawn the yellow curtains.

When the rains ended, did you leave then?

No, not then.

Why not?

I didn't know where to go, did I? And it was very beautiful, after the rains.

So you just stayed there?

What else was I to do? And then one day a man turned up and led me away and I followed. He took me to Hussey.

Just like that.

No, not just like that. We walked for quite a few days, from one village to another. The man pretty much knew where he was taking me. When we got to a new village he always knew of someone there, and we went to that person's hut. Hussey says they have alliances, individual connections they make so that men from one tribe can travel through another tribe's territory. I don't know if it was dangerous, if anyone might have hunted our heads. It didn't seem so dangerous as when we were tracking the Japanese. But there was a place to stay in every village, and other men came to where we were and I think they told my man where to go. Once or twice a man from another village came with us some of the way as a guide. I think it's possible that he didn't even know about the war to start with, and certainly not where to find my people.

All she could see of him was the back of his head. Dark blond hair, a strong neck, his shoulder above the edge of the sheet. He seemed so far from her, just when she felt so close. If she could make him talk then perhaps it would bring them closer. Or perhaps this was just how it was and men always shut in on themselves after sex. She hadn't the experience, she couldn't have said.

It was so dark in those huts that if you had come in from outside you would have scarcely seen a thing. If you woke in one, slept and woke in one, lived in one all of the day, you didn't think of it as dark any more. Only, that all colour was brown.

He had listened for some time before he opened his eyes. The sound was soft, mellow, the rain outside and inside the crackle of fire, the smooth talk of women shot through now and then by children's voices, and all these sounds were already familiar to him, as if he had for some far longer time slipped in and out of listening, between sleep and consciousness, between the nightmare and this. Perhaps he had opened his eyes before, opened and closed them again as he woke and slept, because what he saw when he looked about him did not surprise him. No jungle any more, but this brown hut high above the jungle and above a valley cleared and claimed from the jungle. And in this hut, a hearth, women and children. A young woman squatted before a hearth. A small girl sat beside her with a smaller boy wriggling between her knees, a sturdy round-headed naked boy. Another woman crouched in the shadows behind where he could barely see but clearly hear that she was chopping something on a board. Somewhere out of his vision was an old woman crooning. The boy was the first to notice that he was awake, suddenly looking him in the eye and ceasing to wriggle, watching wide-eyed as he moved to sit up, as he lifted his head, as he took the weight of himself on his elbows; the two things, the stare of the boy and the heaviness of the pieces of his body, bringing him to awareness of his own objective presence, on a hard bamboo bed above the earth floor.

Upright, he could see better. Brown figures, black hair. The hut like an upturned ark. The smoke rising to the roof, to a coaly darkness webbed with soot. The woman at the hearth feeding a piece of branch deeper into the fire. The flames giving a glow to moving skin. He leant his back against a post in the flimsy bamboo wall. She sat sidelong to him so that he could not see her face but only the hair that was heavy and black, and fell forward as she bent to the fire. The boy, still watching him, held a puppy in his arms, but the puppy skipped out of them as a dog came forwards, a pale bitch with distended teats coming to hold the space between this woken stranger and her young. For there were other puppies, he saw, curled together in a mound close by the hearth.

He changed his position. He moved with more noise this time. He needed to exist somehow in all of this, to be recognised by someone other than the boy and the dog. Now they looked round. And at the same moment a baby in the shadows began to cry. Perhaps the sound had been there some time, it had begun as a mewling that he had not recognised at first as that of a child. And the woman from the shadows left off her chopping and took up the tiny baby and sat by the fire to feed it. He felt a kind of relief that it was that woman and not the other, though she looked scarcely any older. The one by the fire was the same girl-woman who had given him rice in the hut in the fields.

They spoke to each other and to him as if there were no language but their own. He understood only the laughter which he knew in their voices and in their eyes if not their smiles. Still he was afraid of the black smiles. They brought him drink, some bitter tea, and rice. Weakly, he bunched the rice in his fingers and began to eat. The children thought this very funny. What was funny? That a white man also ate? Or was it his table manners?

He ate, slept again, dreamt, woke. He was a joke, but perhaps the joke was other than he knew.

There was the constant underlying sound of the fire, the almost constant sound of the rain on the thatch overhead, which varied only in its intensity, and there was laughter. The men running in, wet, shedding at the porch daos and rain shields and soaked blankets, wringing out the blankets, running comic and naked and shivering to the fire as the women moved away to give them space. The puppies scattering before the commotion. The shadow play of grotesques created by the flames as they built up the fire, gargoyle shadows cast by their extraordinary spiky headdresses, shadows that stilled and shrank as the men who made them settled, as they sat to drink rice beer, to fill their pipes, as they began to speak about him. He could see by their gestures that he was the subject of their talk. And they too laughed. They laughed a lot.

He didn't laugh, not at first.

There were skulls hanging on the walls of the hut, and more skulls hung in what he could see of the entrance. They caught whatever light there was, yellow in the firelight, white in the mist-light at the porch, a sheen to bone such as there was to no other substance in the place. Those first days he would be aware all the time of the skulls looking down on him, pale bone and eye-sockets blacker than the women's mouths.

Amazing that one day he would see them only as the ornaments to the house. What would Claire say to that? Let's just run a line of skulls up here, beneath the cornice or along the passage. Or maybe a single one in the fanlight over the front door.

The rain fell harder. There was only a slender bamboo wall between him and the rain, streaming down the thatch, thrashing the ground outside.

She had gone downstairs. He got out of bed and picked up his clothes, went to run himself a bath. The bathroom was chilly and pale, the overhead light too bright. The water poured out loud onto the cast iron.

He bathed quickly as it wasn't hot enough. Went down to join her.

How was your bath?

Lukewarm.

I'm sorry, darling, I must have used too much water for mine.

Waves of rain moved across the village, exposed on its high ridge. At times it sounded to him like the sea. Those first days he thought that it rained without ceasing. He could not say how much time passed. He slept and he woke and it rained. Slowly he recovered but still the days blurred with the rain.

When the rain stopped, time seemed to start up again. The cocks crowed. Even within the hut it lightened. Light penetrated between the woven strips of the walls, pinpoints of light all about the hut, shafts spilling through the umber.

He went out. He looked out to the washed horizon, the violet clouds, the endlessness of the hills. He walked through the village to the men's platforms. Where the cloud had withdrawn the terraces lay revealed like rippled sand when the tide has receded, ripple below ripple as if a whole ocean had pulled back from its green floor.

He saw them going down, women with baskets held by straps across their foreheads, men with daos on their shoulders – hoe and machete and sword all in one so that they might as well have been going to fight as to work. Other groups of men with old muzzle-loaders or boys with catapults went hunting in the forest. A few always stayed behind like himself, watching from the heights the small figures down below, listening to their calls, old warriors who seemed to have earned the right to watch and not to work as the tattoos merged into their ageing skin. At the hut, the oldest remained and the youngest, seated outside now when there was sunshine. They seemed glad to have him join them there, smiling to see his increasing strength. There was only the simplest communication between them, of look and gesture. He tried to pick up what he thought were the words for the commonest things. Water. Tea. Names of foods. He wanted to know the names of the family but they confused him with their variety of names and seeming names, or perhaps some of these were not names but other words meaning sister, brother, mother, girl, boy, baby, little one, darling, sweetheart, so that he was never sure what to call them. As for himself, he did not know if they had a name for him. Sometimes he thought they did, but this too may only have been a term.

My name is Charlie, he said. So they began to call him that. The word sounded quite different on their lips. This Charlie was unlike any Charlie he had been before.

He thought that he knew what the girl was called. Henlong. But then other people called her other things. Could it be that they had more names than one, for the different people they might be? Better if he too were to have more names.

Rain. That was a word he would like to have known. There seemed to be too many words that might have meant rain.

The clouds swept in. It rained. They moved back inside the huts.

Fire. That word too. The fires were kept going all day inside the huts, the smoke filtering up through the thatch. When the rain ceased and he went out, he saw the blue haze of smoke above the thatch as if the whole hut was steaming.

There were looks and signs that were clear indications. This. That. You. Me. And imperative verbs were clear also. Go. Come. Drink. Sleep.

When eventually he got to Hussey, Hussey would want to transcribe all he knew of the language they spoke. Yet he had brought so few words with him. He seemed to have used so few words in all the time that he was there, and many of them he was unsure of, out of context. I think, sir, that this was the word. Or perhaps it was this one. Water, at least, I can tell you the word for water. Does that word occur in any dialect that you know? Does that help you identify the tribe?

But it wouldn't. These days would remain without name or place or time. There would be only immediacies, moments, that would come back to him later as if they were still in the present. The fire, a brown hand reaching forward to tend it, this moment repeated again and again as the logs were pushed deeper into the burning heart and the fire burned on through all the day. The feeding of the tiny baby in the firelight, he sitting so close that in the brightness of the flame he could see the fontanelle pulsing beneath almost transparent newborn skin; it was the soul they saw there, Hussey would tell him, dancing beneath the membrane, only lightly contained within the skull, the soul that was the power for which heads were hunted. And there was the old woman eating slowly, continuing to eat after the others had finished, eating like a cat tiny pawfuls of rice, and yawning after, like a cat, and in the yawn was the soul's impatience to leave its ageing shell of bone.

Then there was the brightness when he stepped outside after the burrow-closeness of the hut. The dazzling blue distance. The girl-woman standing out in the sunlight wearing only strings of beads and the barest strip of a skirt, wiping away with the back of her hand a trickle of blood that seeped down the inside of her thigh.

He, once, must have screamed in the night.

He was awake, bathed in sweat, back in the jungle with the others. A hand came, he did not know whose hand it was, stroked his fear back inside himself until he was whole once more. A voice soothed him with murmured unintelligible words. A body lay alongside his until he slept.

———

I was there some months, he would tell Hussey in the bungalow at Mokokchung. Through the last of the rains and then after the rains ended. I quite lost track of time.

Hussey's bungalow would surprise him with its familiarity, the furnishings and words and flavours which spilled into him like memories and brought him back to who he had been so that he heard his own voice speaking and identified the man that he was, and identified him not only as himself but as an Englishman with a name and a distant home and a regiment. Lieutenant Charles Ashe of the Royal Norfolks, his hand placing a teacup onto a willow-patterned saucer.

If you give me a calendar I suppose I can work it out. So many days in the jungle before I got there, so many days on the trek after, each night in a different village. I was ill at first, feverish, sleeping off and on, probably delirious, perhaps for days on end, I have no idea how long that lasted. There was some kind of medicine woman, some wrinkled old witch, who came and looked at me and prescribed teas made from jungle plants, I don't know what, and I don't know if they had any effect or not, maybe they did, actually I think that they must have had an effect. Or perhaps I would have recovered anyway. The fever came and went, and then it went altogether and I got stronger, and when I was fit to make the walk I started to go down with them and help in the fields.

He would take a cigarette from the box that Hussey offered and sit back and light it as Hussey's servant, a trim silent Naga in white shirt and khaki shorts, put the tea things, one by one and carefully, onto a tray to clear them away. He had not smoked English cigarettes since they first went out on patrol. He paused, closed his eyes to savour the draw and the exhalation.

It's strange, you know, I didn't think about leaving. I just went on, from day to day. One day just followed another, one day very much like another. He felt the hit of the tobacco. He could easily have counted the days, but he hadn't. The only reason to do that would have been if they were wanted or expected to end. Now his hand, the hand of this Englishman that was himself, as it went to tip the ash from the end of the cigarette into the ashtray, began to shake.

Then when did you leave? Hussey would ask. How did it come about?

Hussey held on to his pipe with an earnest look. Hussey smoked a pipe, not cigarettes, held his pipe even when it was not alight, ease in the way he held it, like some housemaster listening to him, Hussey who looked familiar as a master from some minor public school, only the more lined and leaner from years spent not in any English school but out here on trek in these hills. Perhaps Hussey was the one man who might have understood.

What happened then? How did you get here, to me?

It should have been easier to speak to Hussey than to anyone. But already the story was beginning to change shape, the village becoming more distant and exotic, slipping between his words.

A man came from some other tribe.

The smoke moved away from him blue in the sunlight.

Perhaps he came by chance, but I think that they must have sent for him. I left with him the next morning.

There it was. He must hold it down to plain facts.

———

There had been the usual evening in the hut. Every such evening much the same, Hussey would know that. The talk about the fire, as always in the evenings the men closer to the flames, the women receding into the shadows. This particular evening, the rice beer offered around a little more generously on account of the visitor, a thin supple man who wore on his head something like a Viking helmet constructed of cane and bristly black boar's skin and stuck with tusks; but what was most striking about him, in these surroundings, was the fact that he wore oversized British military-issue khaki shorts – it did not bear thinking where he might have rustled them up – and a red blanket such as the British gave to interpreters, though he spoke so very little English.

Good morning, he said, though it was night.

Good morning, Charlie said in reply, and put out his hand, and the slender Viking knew, if somewhat theatrically, how to shake it.

The fire before them. Heat in the fire and light. The darkness behind so deep and close that he felt the touch of it on the back of his neck. The beer was passed around in long bamboo cups. Now and then one of the men took up a thin metal pipe, put it to the fire and blew through it – the sound low and fluting – to bring up the flames. Briefly the shadows lightened. Faces glowed with the drink and the fire. The traveller had tales to tell. His gestures were expressive, his long hands moving across the firelight. The helmet cast a strange horned shadow. Broad white bands of ivory glinted high on his arms. The others listened to his tales, nodded, drank. A man prepared opium to smoke, bringing out a scrap of cloth, melting the opium from it, warming it in a spoon above the fire, the process like a ritual; the blending of the black oil with herbs, the filling of the bamboo water pipe, all done with deft brown priestly fingers; the lighting of it.

The pipe passed from man to man. It came to him and he took it softly as the other men did, drew, paused, passed it on. He listened to their speech, saw their eyes gleaming, watched the fire, felt the darkness at his back.

He knew the darkness and the skulls on the walls behind him, the glare of eye sockets, the grin of broken jaws. The flesh was long gone from them. The dead were dead, far from him now.

He rose and went outside. He felt unseen as if the dark had filled him. No moon that night. The sky clear, the stars very bright but their brightness all in the sky and not on the ground. That was velvety black, mud soft beneath his feet, the long low huts between which he walked shaggy sphinxes holding black space between their paws. Sometimes in the nights he would hear the rustle and pant of couples there where there were benches beneath the eaves, see figures slink beneath the overhang of thatch, and he had walked by with a sense that he himself was no more than a shadow while only they in the darkness were flesh and blood and real. He was no one, a white man, invisible, passing by. And if he was invisible, then the whisper he heard could not be directed at him. Yet the whisper repeated itself. It was a girl's whisper, coming from the darkness. He could not have distinguished whether he knew her first by her whisper or her outline or her touch or her smell. They made love as if it was not the first time at all, as if he had through all these days known what it was to make love to her, her body, her movement, the smoky taste of her, since that first moment when she had given him rice to eat from her fingers.

Home soon, my darling

Really, she might have said, if she had had some other woman there to speak to, to whom she might have attempted to explain how it had come about that she was living this life which did not seem to be her own life but some other woman's. Really, she had known him so little before they were married.

They had met in London, in other people's houses, at parties and in restaurants. They had been attracted from the first moment. They had walked miles on the streets and that was how they had been alone at first, walking side by side and in step and surrounded by others, he with his hand hot to her waist or hers skimming his arm, or in the park when they met in the daytime or in the illusory intimacy of the cinema. How do you know a man in London and then know him all alone, just the two of you, out here where there's no one else? No background, no noise. And not the war there either, thrumming behind all they did. There had been so little thought to getting engaged.

He seemed beautiful to her when he came back. She thought that he must have spent all his days on the ship in a deckchair gazing at the blue. He was thinner, his face thinner so that the structure of it stood out, and he was tanned and his hair had gone very blond which made his eyes the colour of that ocean she thought he had seen and sky. He brought her a present

of an exotic necklace heavy with silver and cornelian beads –
not the kind of thing she'd wear but a lovely thing to handle
and to hang from her dressing-table mirror – and she thought
that he must have brought it back from India and the jungle
but he said no, only from the bazaar in Port Said on the way
home. I was thinking of you, he said. All the way home. I was
thinking of you too, she said, but she did not say how she had
learnt to put the thought away, as one did, as a girl must, in
all that time in which there was no word of him. I knew you
would come back, she said, though it wasn't true, everyone
knew that Burma was bad and a piece of her hadn't expected
him back at all. So here he was, Charlie, when she met him
alone at Southampton, across the glossy dining table when he
came to stay that first night with her parents in Clapham, his
blue eyes looking as if from a distance as he humoured her
father's views on the forthcoming election, holding the silver
knife and fork loose in his long tanned fingers as if none of
it actually mattered, the food, the manners, the appearances,
and he might just let them drop. In the morning they walked
on the lawn in the summer sunshine, before he left to go and
see his mother in the country. Her parents were inside behind
the French windows. He gave her that gift. To her parents
looking out they must have looked like any engaged couple
should have looked, he handing her the gift, the two of them
kissing in the sunshine. If there was some strangeness in the
moment, some sense that even this moment was only loosely
held, then she told herself it was just the strangeness for him
of coming home. It's the war. It's all he's been through, all that
we won't speak of, that the men don't speak about when they
come home, war-illness-battle-jungle-Japs.

That last was the worst, by all accounts. But the war with
the Japs was still going on, you knew it went on even as there
was peace here. You knew that the awfulness continued and
that there would be more to come. And it did come, some

weeks later, a bomb that was more awful than anything that had gone before, and yet when you first heard of it, it seemed a marvel in what it ended; and in the months after that so many other stories seeping in, of prisoners and atrocities – the railway, thank goodness he was spared that. She did say once, almost offhand, sometime much later, the thought slipped out, how the bomb seemed like God's vengeance on the Japanese. Oh no, Claire, he said then, suddenly stiff and fierce as she had never seen him before. Oh no, Claire, you can't say that, don't let me ever hear you say anything like that, you who spent all of the war here, only here, and read it in *The Times*. It was the first time she had seen him angry.

No, she said, her arms tight to her sides, retracting and yet longing at that same moment to hold him. No, you're right, I'm sorry, darling, that was thoughtless of me. She meant that she had been thoughtless not just of the people of Hiroshima and Nagasaki but of him and whatever he must have experienced.

He had recognised her instantly in the crowd, her slight figure distinct even at a distance, even in her hat and big woollen coat. She was so known: her look, the smell of her when they kissed. And yet, not known at all. Her voice was surprising to him yet it must be the same voice it had always been.

Charlie darling, she had said, and kissed him and hugged him tight, and he had felt the neatness of her body against his, her smallness as she reached up to him, and how her hat was dislodged by the kiss. He spoke in return only the plainest things. Hello. Claire. She put up her two hands to rearrange her hat. Where do we go now? London. When does the train leave? Is there time to catch it? On the journey silence could be concealed by the sound of the train. It was only later, when they were there in London in her family's house, that he had unpacked and taken out the necklace he meant to give her, and looked about in himself for things to say.

All her letters had been forwarded when he got to Hussey's at Mokokchung. They had been bundled together wherever the regiment bundled letters for the missing, and came to him with string about them and a blur and a tropical warp to each page from waiting out the rains. Darling Charlie, she wrote. London does look grim in the war. Grim on these winter evenings like when I last saw you, with all the blackout, but grimmer somehow even than during the Blitz because it seems permanent now, it's been so long. Grim on the streets, but so gay inside! For a treat I went to the Criterion with Mary and a gang of friends – Andrew was there, by the way, he says hello, he's been around a while, he was wounded but he's fine now, going back any day – and it was five o'clock on a February afternoon but so bright and gay once you were through the doors. Darling Charlie, Hoping the war is going well where you are. You must have heard, we're in Europe now! I thought it was coming. Mary and Jack stole a weekend away in the West Country before he went back to his ship, and they didn't say right away but Mary told me after how they saw thousands of soldiers there, thousands and thousands of Americans on the move and camped out, everywhere they went, so they knew there was a big push on. Darling, Blast those beastly Japs! The news here is so full of hope, but no news of you! Darling Charlie, I saw a film, *For Whom the Bell Tolls*, Gary Cooper unbearably romantic in Spain, and thought of you, thought I'd write the moment I got home. My darling, Hoping the postal service is on strike in Burma and that's why I don't get any letters, sacks and sacks of envelopes heaped up in the post offices and the Burmese postmen with their feet up on the tables smoking opium or whatever it is they do there. But I hear it's the monsoon. Maybe they all got washed away? Harry Browne spent some time in Burma before the war. He said the rivers are so big you can't see across them. Big brown rivers with waves in them and our letters tossing about like paper boats.

No, Claire, he had wanted to say, you're thinking of a quite different place. Burma is vast. You don't think that when you just look at it on a map. And was he ever in Burma? And how long did he spend in Burma? There was no way of telling where the border was and Burma began. No name to any where. There was only jungle and mountain, and bare slashed mountain and jungle again, and the rivers ran wild in the gorges and you could see across but you could not cross them except where the people had swung their cat's-cradle bridges of vines, which you walked like a dancer, one foot delicate and light before the other.

He had collected the letters at the post office, walked the steep road back up to the bungalow with the bundle unopened in his hand, a burning weight it seemed though it was only paper. He had flicked through the envelopes even as they were tied, and recognised her writing, and his mother's, and saw there were even one or two from Uncle Ralph. He pictured them in England, writing and licking those envelopes and directing them into nothingness. He took the bundle and put it before him on the table on the veranda. He untied the string and took up the paper knife and sliced the softened paper. He read them in the order in which they were piled, which was pretty much backwards in time. If he had read them chrono-logically it might have been different. As it was, the first letters struck him with their brittleness of tone. The words in them seemed false and unreal. And that unreality then ran through, back to the ones which had been written first, when the writ-ers would have had him as a living presence in their minds and written in the confidence that he was alive.

He knew that he must write back. He held the pen in his hand and looked out from where he was writing, from the veranda of this hilltop bungalow, with its familiar details and clipped privet and rose beds, and a view of hills of a height and distance and blueness that he could not begin to convey to someone in England. Would he address the writers of those first letters which he had read last, or the ones who thought him dead? Dear, Darling, Mother, Claire. He wrote openings and no more. Easier perhaps to write to Ralph. Ralph alone might have known how to read what he had written, to read what was behind and could not be said. Ralph knew what one did not say, man to man or man to boy. When he was a boy and his father died, Ralph had crouched before him and put a big slow hand on his shoulder, and that had been better than any words. But he could not write to Ralph without first writing to his mother, that would have upset her if she got to know of it, that he had written to her brother-in-law first instead of her – and his mother needed words. Dearest Mother, I'm fine. Was lost for a while but some tribespeople took me in. Sorry, you must have had a scare there. I'll be on my way home soon. But she would have wanted more than that. She would know all of that already. Hussey had sent a telegram, and there would have been communications from the Army. There was really no need now for letters, he thought. He could thank them for theirs in a simple telegram. That was all the word he would send for now. Better, besides, for putting their minds at rest. Telegrams travelled so much faster. ALL WELL STOP SEE YOU SOON

The telegram could have said more. Was ill. Am better. Could have left sooner. Am in no hurry to leave. Can't tell you why.

In Calcutta he began again. My darling Claire, I'm on my way at last. At a desk in the foyer of a great hotel that reminded him of Piccadilly he started his letter. Perhaps it would be easier to write now that he was halfway. Now he had a sheet of fine formal English headed paper beneath his fingers. My dearest Claire, There's so much to say, I don't know where to begin. There was a clatter from the dining room that was entirely British, a sound of Piccadilly and white china and linen tablecloths and heavy silver-plated cutlery bearing the crest of the hotel, which also appeared on the headed paper. The letter wasn't likely to get home much sooner than he did, but he went on writing, trying to find the voice in which he spoke to her, whatever voice it was he had at home. It's so strange, to think that I'm coming home and will see you in only a matter of weeks. I hope you'll find me not too much changed. A bit thinner, of course, but I've got rid of the beard so you should recognise me at least. Had a haircut too. Not sure you'd be too impressed with the Indian barber, but there's a bit of time for it to grow before we meet. And he imagined then some meeting like a meeting in a film, he disembarking, looking for her in the crowd, and now he could not picture her face. Memory could be so precise on some things, so vague on others. He thought that one of the Englishwomen in the hotel had a look of her, in the way her dark hair curled to her neck, the way she moved, a slim waist on which he might put his hand; but then he thought that in some way all of the young Englishwomen here seemed to look the same. Perhaps it was an effect of the cotton dresses they wore, and the hats and the lipstick; or perhaps it was something that India did to them, making them generic, and at home they would become more distinctly themselves. Would that be so? If she came to the docks to meet him, would he be able to tell her apart from the rest?

This time too he would settle for a telegram. There was a telegraph counter with clocks on the wall above it: the time in Cairo, Paris, London, New York. He wrote just a few words standing at the counter: EMBARKING CAL FOURTH MAY STOP TELL ALL WHEN I SEE YOU STOP LOVE CHARLIE. When he turned from the telegraph desk he found himself face to face with one of those women.

Charlie, isn't it? We met at Dickie Wilton's. It's Julia, Julia Esmond. Funny to see you here, well, marvellous actually. I suppose you're surprised to see me too, but the war does that, doesn't it, makes strange meetings? What are you doing in Cal?

He saw her lipsticked mouth babbling gaudy words, her blue eyes so sure of him, of that sociable amusing Charlie she thought she recognised.

I'm sorry, he said, I don't think I know you.

In that moment it was true. Even if some part of him did remember her, that made no difference.

The ship went through Suez. Ashore at Port Said he bought her a present. It was what men did, going home. They went to the bazaar in the last exotic place they visited and rifled through trinkets and silks and jewels because they understood almost too late that they must take back to those who loved them some sign that they had been remembered so far away. That was what Port Said was for, surely, a place for Europeans to pretend, a desert city built only to serve their shining canal. He saw others like himself walking in khaki or in linens through oriental hubbub, lying to themselves that they had seen and known other than they had seen, thinking that they must bring back some evidence of what they were supposed to have seen to those at home who had not seen and who had missed them. The necklace caught his eye. It had a particular beauty, nothing of the trinket about it. He took it up and liked the unexpected weight of it in his fingers, bought it for a sum of money that he negotiated with no notion of its provenance or worth, whether it had been newly made and antiqued in some back street there in the city or was a hundred years old and had come a thousand miles on a camel. He took the necklace away in his pocket in a little bag of red and gold silk, and went back to the ship, and once he was down in his cabin he laid it on the bed and unstrung the bag and looked again. It looked alien now that he saw it outside the bazaar. And wrong. The only jewellery he could picture her wearing was pearls. Wasn't that what Julia Esmond and those other women he had so recently seen who were like her liked to wear? But the necklace was what it was, and the ship was about to embark; he could hear the hum of the engines through the cabin floor.

He gave it to her in the garden. The lawn was freshly mown.

He was aware of the scent of grass and the stripes.

It's lovely, she said. Rather savage.

She held the necklace before her. She had smooth skin, fine collarbones, dark eyes. If she were to wear it, it might suit her better than pearls.

Thank you, darling.

Her voice set her apart from him in a way that the touch and the smell of her did not. Her words rang in some bright space within him and made him feel in that moment that he was hollow.

Did it come from India?

I got it in Port Said. We stopped there *en route*.

A gust of wind blowing her veil, stepping out into the unexpected. Yet it should have been expected. None of it was so surprising, really.

But you don't know the country, he had said when they first talked about marriage. You've never lived in the country.

They had been walking in Green Park. It was the greenest place they had been in all the time they had known each other, the London planes above their heads and the grass beneath their feet.

I did. In my last years at school. They sent us away to a school in Wiltshire because of the Blitz.

That's not the same as living there.

And I picked potatoes. They sent us out potato picking in our games lessons instead of playing hockey. So I've even done some farming, you see. Thought I might be a Land Girl, but when I got back to London I joined the ATS instead.

Lucky you did that.

Why?

We'd never have met, would we, if you'd been a Land Girl, stuck out on some farm somewhere?

They lay on the grass and kissed, but chastely, because of where they were. His uniform was rough to her hands.

Some silly idea she had then of the life she would lead, knowing Charlie, knowing about his family and the house – the big house that was sold and the farmhouse that Uncle Ralph had kept on with the land, which was meant for Charlie to inherit. Charlie said that it was a lovely old house though it was only the home farm, much easier to live in than the big house, with a couple of formal rooms at the front and views out in all directions over the fields. The family had been there for generations. Their name appeared on memorials in the church. She would take that name, become a part of all that. One day – but not now, not yet, not until she had lived there some time and was rather older – she pictured herself walking to the church, on a Friday it might be, or a Saturday afternoon, with armfuls of flowers, and arranging them there, daffodils or lilac or roses, or autumn leaves and berries, before the pulpit or about the font. She pictured herself more of a country lady than a farmer's wife. She would do whatever country ladies did, walk a dog, have a garden, grow those flowers.

They were in the cottage at first. Temporarily. It had been easy to be temporary, as if they were only playing at their life together. The cottage was halfway down the drive. It had small rooms, small windows, and it was chilly, with a fireplace that smoked, so they turned in early and warmed themselves in a creaking bed that must she thought have been built in the room. She could not imagine how anyone could have brought such a big bed up the stairs.

When Ralph died they moved to the farmhouse but it was still Ralph's house to her. She felt no more permanent than she had in the cottage. Morning after morning she walked downstairs like a guest when Charlie was already up and out, keeping what poor Ralph had used to call 'London hours'. She thought to hear Ralph's voice as she walked in her pink dressing gown down the stairs past sporting prints in their dark wood frames, hunting scenes, hounds and men on horses, running foxes, horses jumping hedges.

Charlie worked long days in those first months. She had had to do the move without him. Not that they had so many things to move but only their clothes and bedding from the cottage, and the wedding presents, many of which were still in their original packing, glasses and china and cutlery and two toasters, and a silver cigarette box, but Ralph had had almost all of those things. It had been more a question of moving his things out, or moving them around, than moving theirs in. Her mother came to visit to help. It was a sombre move, into a dead man's house, yet the two of them went about it with hope. They opened the windows all round, the sash windows at the front pushed right the way down, and the house breathed in the summer air and the sound of the pigeons came from the trees. They cleaned first. They had Mrs Tuckwell, who had done the housekeeping for Ralph, for two full days, and her daughter Elsie who was on her holiday from school. They began in the kitchen. It seemed important to begin there. Sometime soon it would have to be modernised, an electric cooker put in, the butler's sink replaced, the pipework redone that ran to it exposed across the window; the flagstone floor that was so cold, so unforgiving when you dropped a plate, covered perhaps with lino. They spoke of the modern kitchens they had seen in magazines as they cleared and scrubbed and relined drawers and shelves, and threw out old spices and handle-less saucepans and cracked bowls.

When they had done the kitchen the four women moved on about the house, taking separate rooms. She left Ralph's study to Mrs T and Elsie. Just pile the papers, she said. Neatly so that they can be gone over later. Don't throw anything away for now. The important thing is just to get the desk clear. What about the drawers? Mrs T asked. The desk was a big one with a worn leather top and drawers all the way down on each side.

Yes, let's do those, Claire said, fired up with the activity, and she knelt and pulled open one drawer after another, papers and letters and pens, and Ralph's old spectacles, and a broken pipe with a smell of tobacco that seemed like the smell of him. I'll give you a box to put everything in. Then she saw that Mrs T was crying, in her floral apron leaning with her knuckles on the desk. No, no, I'm sorry. Leave the drawers for now. Let's leave the drawers. And leave all that mess on the shelves around the gun rack, Charlie can sort all that out. Let's just do the surfaces. Elsie, maybe you can start with the papers? We'll need some boxes anyway, I'll go and get some. And she went to the corridor at the back of the house where they had put the empty boxes in which the wedding presents had come, and found that she was weeping too.

Ralph's presence in the sitting room was less obvious. It looked like the room of anybody of that type and class.

This could be a lovely room, her mother said, standing before the open windows. Her mother had met Ralph only once, at the wedding. It's so light and airy, south-facing, it only needs a lick of paint. And some new curtains, she went on, fingering the sage-coloured damask where the threads had worn through in the sunlight.

She looked at her mother standing there with the motes of dust about her. Ralph's dust, she thought. She heard the pigeons outside. It did not rain all of that August after they moved in and there was the scent of the harvest and the constant sound of the pigeons, and she was envious of Charlie who spent all of these days outside.

And chair covers, perhaps, she said, pulling herself in.

Yes, chair covers, of course. Let's go shopping when you come up to London, see what we can find.

She didn't know how much she dared dislodge. There were china figurines on the mantelpiece, Marie-Antoinette shepherdesses whose backs were reflected in the wide gilt mirror, a carriage clock set between them, Ralph's watercolours on the walls. I like the watercolours, she had said, Ralph collected those. Those must stay. Perhaps we should paint the walls a pale shade to set them off, what do you think?

You should move the pictures out of the sun if they're good. Or keep the curtains drawn. They get too much sun in here.

Her mother was right, of course. It would be some time before they did anything with the room. Even the shepherd-esses had not moved except to be dusted, and when Mrs T had done the room and gone, Claire would rearrange them, placing them so that they might regard their reflections side-long, slightly differently, each week. But she had listened to her mother's advice and left the curtains drawn to protect the pictures when they weren't using the room, though that made it a gloomy room to enter.

All of the house was gloomy on a November morning. Again, she was keeping London hours. She had heard Charlie moving when she was half-asleep. She might have gone downstairs and made breakfast but she could not face the half-light. She did not get up until she had heard the trac-tor start. She dressed, quickly because the room was cold. Though she could see the steps perfectly clearly, she put on the lights as she went downstairs, on the landing and on the stairs and in the hall, because she needed lights where Charlie when he had gone down had not. With the lights on, colour began to live, that didn't exist with only the grey of the outside that came through the windows, the touches of colour that she had introduced to the house, a pretty bowl or a set of cushions, bright new tea towels in the kitchen, those tiny changes she had made that marked her presence here.

Let her keep her London hours. He had known she was awake but he had crept out all the same. This had been a bachelor house. In this house there was the habit of a man getting up alone, filling the stove, making breakfast for himself. Not that it was that early. The days were short now. It was getting on for eight by the time he had the tractor out. There were three fields at the end of the farm that Ralph had always ploughed first. The soil was heavier there than elsewhere. If you didn't get on to them before Christmas, Ralph had said, you might not be on to them until late in the spring. There had been rain the previous week but the weekend had been dry. He hoped that the ground would be crisp enough to work despite the lack of wind.

It was still slimy on the track. He knew before he got there that it would be too wet. He persisted as if the noise of the tractor and the judder of it beneath him were purpose alone, the exhaust chimney above the engine puffing blue smoke into the grey. He cut a first slow line into the field where he had left off before the rain. It was a waste of time. As Ralph would no doubt have told him. Patience, boy. Ralph touching his sleeve. Ralph who taught him how to ride and shoot, and whatever he knew about how to farm. Take your time. Everything has its time. Don't push things. Take a good look at the land first.

Billy had said pretty much the same thing in the yard the day before. It'll be stubborn as hell, Billy had said. You c'n afford to wait.

When there were only horses, Billy had said, they would never have dreamt they could be this far on before the end of November. Tractors made a man impatient.

He said it again when Charlie drove back to the yard, calling him the boss but making him feel like a boy. And then he went on, and he could not tell if it was irony he saw in the old man's so honest-seeming face. But you can't be that sure, can you, sir? Never know, sir, could be it'll rain every day now till Christmas.

Billy and Joseph were going to start the winter work on the hedges. That was good work for a day like this. The three of them walked the farm speaking of where to begin. He left them coppicing the hazel by Long Field and walked alone back to the yard, his boots heavy with mud so that the field seemed ever the longer, the sky unrelievedly grey above the black roofs of the barns. The leaves sagged from the trees, dulling from gold now to sodden brown. He would go back later and work alongside them the rest of the day, he thought, and those that followed, until he could get back onto the land.

Come, Jess, let's go find Charlie. The retriever jumped up from the basket by the stove, crowded about her as she put on her coat, too big a dog for the narrow passage to the back door, almost tripping her up. Why such excitement to go into the bare cold fields? She took the lead from the hook by the door and put it in her pocket in case they went near the cows. She didn't know where he would be.

She walked out to where she had seen him ploughing those few days earlier, before the rain, saw where he had started on the next field and given up. The dog ran off on a scent.

She saw the smoke of the fires and walked towards it, found the men. They were cutting the hedge and were burning the brush, cutting and feeding the fires in turn, two fires set a distance apart along the field edge. Charlie had his coat off. He was handsome and flushed from the work, and the heart of the fire was hot.

What are you doing?

The hedges are overgrown. No one paid much attention to them in the war.

Oh. There was so much she had never thought of: how this countryside was shaped, the hedgerows and the woods as well as the fields, all of it, had had to be shaped and managed and made.

He pulled over a cut branch, added it to the flames. Billy builds a good fire, he said. Even after the rain and with all this elder. Elder's a beast to burn.

Can I work with you? He looked so happy with the work, so much himself. She had a sudden urge to be part of it too, of the work and the heat. She envied the men their work and their wordless companionship, their companionship with each other and with all the men who had worked this hedge and this land before them.

You'll need some better gloves than that. Here, take mine.

What about you?

My hands are tough.

Thick leather gloves big on her hands, already warm inside from his. Clumsy. She went to where Billy was cutting and began with the smaller branches, dragging them over and piling them on, moving about the fire away from the smoke.

Billy had pulled out a great knot of dry dead bramble. You better be taking that, madam, as you've got the gloves. See how bright that goes.

A whoosh of yellow and blue flames went up from the bramble soon as it touched the fire. She jumped backwards from the heat.

How lovely! she said. Then she felt frivolous for saying that in front of the men, as if she was at a party or something.

A simple supper as she had been out so much of the day.

Let's go somewhere tomorrow, Charlie said. Take a trip somewhere, if I still can't get onto the land.

Where?

Where would you like to go?

She thought of the gulls that had not come in these last days of wet. Let's go to the sea, she said.

The gulls had come like the wild over the land whose bareness she found so oppressive. Grey and white like pieces of sea themselves.

Yes, he said. Let's do that.

He had got up to put his plate by the sink, but he came back suddenly behind her and put his two hands on her hair and kissed the top of her head between them.

Your hair smells of bonfire, he said, and put his nose to it.

The scent was there that night in the bed with them.

Let's go out tomorrow, whatever the weather. Leave Billy and the rest to do whatever there is to do on the farm. Let's go early, have the whole day.

Glad you made it out

If we're going to the coast, darling, and if it's not too far, we should go and see your friend Walter's family. If you don't mind me coming with you. You do keep saying that you mean to visit them. Or if you want to see them alone then I suppose I could sit in the car. I wouldn't mind, just so you got to see them.

So they were going to Holkham.

———

I know it, he had said, when Walter had first named the estate where he worked. It's a beautiful place. I went there once or twice.

He remembered the woods, and the beach, which was longer and sandier than any other on this stretch of coast. There was marsh along much of the coast, but not there, there the beach ran directly up to the trees.

He had visited Holkham when he was boy, in the holidays when he was sent to stay with Ralph. That was one of the things that made him close to Walter, when they discovered it soon after they met. I know your uncle Ralph, Walter said. A fine shot, your uncle Ralph.

Every keeper in the county must have known Ralph. It was Ralph who had pushed him to join up with the Norfolks. He had served with the Norfolks himself, in the First War. He had come home badly wounded – no good to women, as he said, after what Jerry did – and put the rest of his life into the farm, a limping, amiable, bachelor farmer who must have been invited to every shoot in the county. If Charlie had seen Walter among the keepers at Holkham, he had no memory of it. It had been different then. Then they were boy and keeper. Once they were in the jungle they were only men even if there was a rank between them.

He should have gone sooner. He could have made the trip soon as he got back to England. He might have taken the train from London for the day. At least he might have gone in the spring when they came to the farm. It was only twenty miles, an easy drive now he made it, a slow weave cross-country through villages and down minor roads.

A few drops of rain showed on the windscreen and for an instant he set the wiper going.

I do hope it's not going to rain, she said.

The cloud's still quite high. I don't think it'll rain hard.

Such a mild day today, not like November at all.

Dull land it was on such a day, this land of big estates and big shoots: wide verges to the roads, hedges and stands and woods and strips of cover planted between rectangular fields, flat functional land in which whatever appeared to be wild was only kept wild for sport. They came to an American airbase and the road diverted around it. Such great areas of farmland had been given over to the war. He wondered how long they would remain, the Americans and the runways and the hangars and the huts.

We'll go to the house first and then walk. If she's not in then we can leave a note and walk first and go back later.

Are you sure she'll be there?

Shouldn't think she's gone anywhere.

He had written a letter from Mokokchung, from Hussey's bungalow. He had written the usual kind of letter, the usual words about gallantry but not those final ones that were wanted, about wherever he was buried. The absence of such words glared out from the page. He had written the letter a dozen times and there had been nothing he could say to fill that space. He wrote how Walter was a fine, brave, imperturbable soldier. How the younger soldiers looked up to him. How everyone looked up to him. He had led them in the jungle. His sons could grow up proud of their father. If only he could have followed that with the final offer of a grave for them to visit, or at least that they might know was there; some notion of a cross bearing his name, some piece of him on that hillside where they were making the cemetery, at Kohima, on that same ground where the battle had been fought.

Won't it be a tied cottage, if he was a gamekeeper? If there's a new gamekeeper then she might have had to leave.

I don't know about that. She said I'd always be welcome. She didn't say anything about going anywhere.

A woman's careful curly script on a small sheet of lined paper. Thank you for your kind letter. We know our Walter was a brave good man. We looked up where you were on the map. It is hard to picture as it is so far off. Please come and see us so that we can know something about it. You will be welcome here at any time.

The house was the last in a row of estate cottages, dark brick with slate roofs, a length of garden in front that was ragged with autumn, Michaelmas daisies fallen along the path. He thought he might tell her how when they were in the jungle Walter had looked up at the trees and spoken of bringing her an orchid home.

It was a boy who answered the door.

She'll be back dinnertime.

We'll come later then.

The boy puzzled, looking at them, at the car. He was small and freckled and dark-haired, nothing like Walter.

He said who he was before the boy had to ask. That would give her time to prepare.

They drove down a track to the beach, parked where the track came to an end facing the sea. The beach was pale sand, wide and long, trees dark to one side of it, slow pewter sea to the other, the grey of the sea paling to the horizon so that there was only a white line of dissolve at last between water and sky. They walked along close to where the waves were breaking. When they had gone some way from the car a fine drizzle began, so fine that it scarcely wet them, only the moisture like dew in her hair as she took out a woollen headscarf from her pocket and tied it over. They came to the broken black posts of some old breakwater and stopped there. The dog ran on but they turned back together, naturally, as if they had reached some unspoken destination. The dog would soon enough turn and follow, catch up with them again.

She saw the sheen of rain on his eyelashes and face. She pulled on her gloves, and saw his hands hide in his pockets where she might not touch them, not touch him, his eyes away on the sand before them and the sea.

The wet in the air seemed quite some other substance from that in the sea, and yet when it fell into the sea the distinction was gone.

His hands in his pockets, his eyes on the edge of the waves, he began again to speak.

After the battle, there was a Naga boy who came out of the forest. The fighting was over. The Japs were gone. The whole town was destroyed, up to the forest's edge, even parts of the forest around it destroyed, broken trees beyond the broken huts. This boy came out like an apparition from where the devastation ended, a thick green jungly wall from which you might have thought only some scavenging animal might emerge, out from between the leaves and creepers.

I saw him from a distance, just happening to glance over that way, a small moving figure where everything had seemed either wild or dead. He walked straight out from that jungle into the battlefield as if he was going somewhere, self-possessed and deliberate like a child walking to school or walking back home after school, and he didn't stop until he came close to where we were working. I had the sense that he knew precisely where he was. Perhaps that was what he was doing, he was going home, perhaps this was where his house had been, or his school.

He must have been the age of that boy we just met, seven or eight, I should think. Or perhaps a little older, if he was a Naga, as the Nagas tend to be small. They'd been living in the jungle all through the battle. They'd fled there right at the beginning and they'd been there for months, and slowly now they were coming out to find what was left of their homes and their land. I don't know why this boy was alone. I kept looking back where he had come expecting some others, expecting his family to follow. He was a skinny little chap as I don't think they'd had much to eat through all of that time, with very black hair in a pudding-basin cut – they have very shiny black hair, the Nagas – wearing nothing but a pair of too-big khaki shorts and a necklace of red and yellow beads.

———

She was attentive as if he had a whole story planned to tell her.

He paused, fell back a step, turned to look for the dog. It was a bit of war one didn't mention. One mentioned battle-fields but one didn't explain what was there. What was there already when they arrived, what had massed there all through the siege, what the burial details were doing as the Army began to grind on ahead.

The battle was won, the story would go, and the Army moved on, without a word for the rest of it. Even at the time the men had done the work almost without speaking. Here. This one. Take up that boot. Looks could say those things as well as words. Handkerchiefs over noses and mouths. They smoked bidis. Those pungent Indian cigarettes worked better than anything else at covering the smell. You did not know if they should be thankful for the rain. Better perhaps rain than sun for work such as this. Rain washed down them, and washed each body as it was buried. Each body was washed as it was buried. Under the rain, identity dissolved. There was only one colour. Every skin, every uniform, the colour of the earth itself. Japs recognisable by their puttees, the Punjab regiments by their turbans. Japs to a mass grave. British to go to individual graves. Colonials to be sorted by religion; Muslims, Sikhs, Hindus, Christians, each to his own grave. A tag handed to a man at a desk in a tent, collected and recorded, name, rank and regiment, with the rain hammering on the roof of the tent louder than it hammered on the mud. You stood at the entrance of the tent and smoked another stinking bidi before going out again into the wet, and you did not know if it mattered who was who and who went where, only that it was decent that each man was put under the ground and not left upon it, and when the bidi was dead between your fingers you threw the tiny stub of it down into the mud. You saw a padre go by and say a prayer. So many graves there were, and many of them nameless, and one of them might have been made for Walter, a long grave for a long stooped Norfolk man. But Walter was still alive then, his thin face solemn, rainwater running down the hollows in his cheeks. He was jumping ahead in time.

If Walter's wife were to ask, could he lie to her?

Perhaps he could, if he had Walter's grave in his mind. He knew precisely how it would look. It would look like those other graves they had dug later in the jungle – that they had dug so fast, looking over their shoulders, listening even as their spades thudded into the mud, shallow graves hastily made to be more hastily covered over, but deep enough for respect, for honour. A long narrow grave in wet jungle soil, tendrils like hairs along its sides and thicker white roots cut through by his spade. Trees for mourners. Mist moving across and turning the bare trunks and the one man standing into shadows, pouring down into the hole to blanket the body at its base.

Would it make it easier, if he were to lie? Or he might more truthfully speak of the cemetery they had left behind them before they went into the jungle, the memorial that was to be built and dedicated to those without bodies or names, from the battle itself or the days that followed. He might tell her how neat it was becoming when he made his return months later, when the rains were over and things were growing again. He could tell her how the new-made crosses ran across the curve of terraced hillside where the DC's bungalow had been and where the worst of the battle had been fought, across the DC's garden and his tennis court; and how it was green already, becoming a garden again. Yes, he should speak of that, the garden.

———

But Claire had waited for him. She wanted him to go on with whatever he had been saying.

The boy had bare feet. The Naga boy was treading so neatly, barefoot, between the bodies.

He remembered looking down at the boy's feet in the mud.

As the dog came to them he picked up a piece of driftwood, automatically, and threw it away ahead. It landed where a wave came in and licked it, and Jess caught it as the wave receded, her tail wagging in the foam.

Small feet. Living feet. Mud squeezed between the toes, spatters of mud on his legs. The softness of his steps in the mud. The quiet of him.

93

Knowing that all this wasn't right. That they were here, that they had done this to his world.

———

He spoke again, now that her eyes were on him. It was some thought about Walter that got him started telling her this.

At some point, close to us as I say, this boy stopped, and he began to look around, as if he'd lost his bearings, or as if he had got to wherever he was going and found it gone, and wondered where to go to next. Walter called then and waved him over. I knew Walter had a family but I hadn't much thought about it till then, that he was somebody's father, father of three boys in fact. So the boy came up to us, and he had this odd solemn poise, and Walter stooped and smiled, Walter had a kind smile, and put his hand to the boy's shoulder and found a sweet to give him, a toffee in its wrapper, and the boy took the sweet without a word but didn't eat it and only put it in the pocket of his shorts, and walked on down the hill, through the death and the debris and the blasted trees, and he was looking about him as if it was all very curious, the whole thing, Walter and the rest of us and the toffee and the bodies. He was the first, but he wasn't the only one. We saw more of them in the days that followed, Nagas coming out of the jungle to look, singly or in groups, walking, only walking. Old men, women, children, women carrying babies in their arms. I didn't think they should be there. Well they're headhunters, somebody said. But they were just sightseeing. They weren't hunting any heads.

I couldn't tell you what they were doing, Claire, they were just looking about them. They had known this place before, however it was before. I don't know, I suppose, perhaps, they were looking for their homes.

———

He saw a woman pick up the white silk of a parachute. At points in the siege supplies had been dropped by parachute. There were clusters of them on the ground here and there, like mushrooms where they had landed and dirtied now to the colour of mushrooms. This woman bent and pulled at the silk, and a light breeze got beneath and made it billow as she pulled it in towards herself. She was small and determined, a matronly little woman in a dark sarong. She wants it for herself, he thought, she will make of it a tent or a dress – or a shroud, a shroud for all of them – as she went on pulling the silk out of the mud, bundling it against her chest. But once she had it all in her arms she let the bundle drop. He had not noticed that the remnants of a hut lay beneath.

———

It was beginning to rain harder now. They got to the car just in time. It was too soon to go back to the house so they sat in the car for a while watching the rain fall, Jess thrashing about as Claire reached awkwardly behind and rubbed her coat dry with the blanket they kept on the back seat.

Darling, you've never told me so much before.

No, I haven't, have I?

He had told her this but he could not begin to convey to her the whole. Number and extent. The smell of it, the maggots, the flies, the rats, the vultures and the crows. The unimaginable panorama, all this going on and on, turning through 360 degrees. The rain, the cloud, the endless ranges of hills that they knew were there even when they could not see them.

He slammed his hand flat to the steering wheel so that the horn sounded out across the beach.

Why there, why were we all there? Of all the places in the world. We'd come all that way to this remotest of places to kill one another, across half the world, we and the Japs – no, not just we and the Japs, but Welshmen, Indians, Gurkhas, Africans with insignia of crossed assegais on their shoulders, each of us distinguishable only by these details once we lay in the mud, and all the same to them. (Sikhs with turbans, the image recurring and recurring, but that he could not say.) How strange it must have been to them that it was their land to which these strangers had come to die, where hardly any strangers had ever come before. It didn't strike home till then. Till then the only Nagas we'd seen were the porters. That was different. They were working for us. They were part of the war.

Thank goodness she didn't speak, because nothing she could have said would have helped. She would know, as he knew, that it wasn't like him to speak like this, not Charlie. She was just looking out now, watching the rain on the glass. He thought of those crazy grinning men, running up for the next load, one after another, as if war was a lark. Who maybe even won them the battle, carrying supplies over the mountain through the siege, along jungle trails and up impossible slopes. Bent backs, wiry legs. Little and cheery and hard and wiry like Tommy Prosser, who had been a stable lad at Newmarket and used to ride the horses out, who might have been a jockey by now if it hadn't been for the war. Racing off as if from the starter's gun. Wonder how they'd run on the flat, Tommy said. Shouldn't think they've seen a piece of flat ground in their lives.

Rain streaked down the windscreen and the windows. Inside, the glass steamed up, with the condensation of their breath and that of the panting dog, and the wet on the dog's hair and on their clothes. The sea began to disappear, and the beach, grey and beige horizontal smears dissolving. She turned to look at him and saw that his eyes were closed. His hands still gripped the wheel. She wanted to touch his face that was still as rock, reach soft fingers to his cheek, to make him open his eyes and turn towards her. She lifted up a hand but his stillness deterred her and she let it drop.

From their post in the Naga Village they had looked steeply down onto a road. That was where they had been stationed when they came to the battle. Sometime early on, perhaps the day they had got there, a Jap had been killed by a sniper on the road. He was still there days later, flat in the mud, flattened deeper into the mud as the battle moved on and the tanks and the vehicles passed along the road. In time he became only the flattened outline of himself, until one morning he wasn't there any more, his disappearance completed with a slow mechanical logic.

Thank God for that, Walter had said. Poor bastard's gone at last.

The jungle seemed a purity when they first volunteered for the patrol. A chance to step away in an instant from the men and the machines and the murder. To disappear beyond the green wall from which that boy had come. To enter into his world which was a world of mist and of filtered green light, to know the depths and varieties and intensities of greenness fed by the rain, to listen to the sound of rain on leaves, on one layer of leaves beneath another, hard leaf to frond to fern, this dripping of moisture the life-flow of the forest, the mist rolling through like its breath. It was as if they had entered a place still evolving, the water still to drain away to make of it an Eden, but the water had not drained yet, it was not ready for their presence, not ready for them, they with their boots and guns an oddity, an intrusion of the future. The things that belonged were the leeches and other creatures of the wet, and eerie birds that they did not see but only heard calling. It was not until later that he would discover what kind of Adam it was who might live there, how such a man moved and spoke and found his way, and found what wild fruits he might eat and an orchid to put behind his ear.

How odd it was, that they should have been left in such a place, they too left to melt into the soil, Englishmen where they did not and would never belong.

———

Charlie darling, It's half past twelve. I should think she'll be back by now.

He reached into his pocket for the key, put it into the ignition and for a moment held it there. He started the car and then, with the engine running, wiped irritably at the inside of the windscreen with his hand so that he could see, as if he had only just noticed the misting, wiping clear just a patch of windscreen in which to see as he turned the car, back and away from the beach.

What would you like me to do, darling? Should I stay in the car?

He turned the car roughly, running onto the verge. She was right. She didn't need to be there. It wasn't her concern.

No, please come, he said. It'll be easier if you're there.

A pine tabletop scrubbed almost white. Tea put out with busy hands: biscuits overlapping on a rosy-patterned plate, milk jug, sugar bowl, saucers, cups, then the teapot and a knitted cosy over it.

Hazel, her name was in the letter, Hazel Clarke. She was short, a little plump, fresh-faced, with brown hair and eyes like the boy they had met at the door, sure in her movements and her speech. She seemed more sure than Claire had expected her to be, a woman who seemed well capable of bringing up three boys on her own. Signs of them were tidied into corners of the kitchen, a jam jar crammed with crayons and some schoolbooks on a shelf, shirts folded by the ironing board, muddied boots on the mat by the door. The room had some deep familiarity to it that she envied. She had not expected to envy this woman anything. (Or perhaps she was not so sure, after all, she would think with hindsight, perhaps she was not really seeing her; she was an outsider here, looking from the outside and with the gulf of class between them, deceived by the plainness of the woman's manner and the homeliness of her surroundings.) She made some compliment, that she hoped came across right and did not sound condescending, what a welcoming house it was to come to when it was raining so hard outside, though in fact the rooms in the cottage were cramped and dim, only the daylight in them and so little of that this particular morning.

It's what keepers' cottages are meant for, isn't it, Hazel Clarke said. For men to come into out of the rain.

Of course, she said. Of course that was so.

It was clear Mrs Clarke had been looking out for them, since she had come to the door as soon as the car drove up. There wouldn't be many cars that stopped before this isolated row of cottages.

You want to be bringing the dog in?

No, no, she's very wet, she'll be fine in the car.

We can have her in, put her in the scullery.

No, really, she's fine. We can't stay long.

She'll dry off better indoors.

Oh you're very kind.

She had taken their coats. Shaken the wet from them, hung them in the passage.

You'd think the weather could've held off for the morning at least, if you've come all this way.

Then she made the tea and they drank the tea, and Claire asked about the boys, their names and ages and schooling, and for a time the two women filled the dim minutes with chat without meaning, as the man was silent, while the rain began to clear outside and sunlight at last to break through, spilling in through the little window and brightening the objects on the table. It seemed as if they might have gone on with their small talk until the visit was over yet the thing that had brought them might not have been mentioned at all.

We looked in the atlas, Hazel Clarke said all of a sudden, turning to Charlie. In that moment she sat very still, and her stillness was heavy in the room. The shaft of light striped the table before her. Me and the boys. Took us a while to find the place.

Yes, he said. It was like the ends of the earth.

That's how Walter put it, in a letter he wrote us. He said he'd come all that way and there were armies from everywhere, but what they'd come to was the ends of the earth.

So you got his letters, I'm glad you got his letters.

He wrote after the battle. He said it was a terrible battle.

It was, but we were all right, Charlie said. The worst was over before we got there. We were just mopping up.

How awkward he looked, Claire thought, as he said that. His hand seemed too big for the fragile cup that he held, though it was empty and he might have put it down.

Perhaps you can show me where you were. Then I can show the boys.

She took a big black atlas down off the shelf where the schoolbooks were, and brought it to the table, clearing a space before him, pushing aside the teapot and the jug and the dish that she had put out such a brief time before, saying how she was glad of the light as it would be the easier to read. The book fell open where it must have been opened many times: India, the British Possessions all pink.

He placed the cup on the saucer, delicately as if the china might shatter.

See, here, he said, up in the north-east, here's Assam. It was a long journey there, Walter must have written to you about that. We disembarked at Bombay, and then we had to go right across the country, all the way up here, to this railway station, up here in the Brahmaputra Valley, and the place was pretty much nothing but a railway station, the name told you that, Manipur Junction, that was all that mattered about it, that it was on the railway, and there we set off for the hills. Kohima's marked. You found Kohima?

So many names, but he didn't know the use of them; just a list of places passed through, where they'd not stopped and nothing had occurred. Why did he see the need to tell her all of these names?

And then, she wanted to know. She said the words plainly but he saw how her hands were clenched into fists on the table by the book's edge. And then, after that, where did they go after that? This was what she had wanted to know, not any of the rest. The rest she could have worked out for herself.

After that, we followed the Japanese retreat. Most of the force went south, this way, along the road towards Imphal, and then east towards the Chindwin, and detachments spread out into the mountains.

She looked where his finger pointed as if there was something actually to be seen in the smooth and empty pink.

Here, they're marked up here, the Naga Hills. They run on to the south, but the map doesn't show you that. The map has it all one colour. It doesn't show you how mountainous it is there, this whole area a chaotic tract of mountains running on from India into Burma. We were here, somewhere along the red line that shows the border. Even here it's printed in parts as a dotted line. Parts of it haven't even been charted.

He had no more names to tell her because there weren't any to be told.

You mean no one had been there before?

Oh, there are people there, just not Europeans.

But he had told her nothing, only geography. He knew that he must say something more. Why make the visit, if he had nothing to tell her?

All the chaps looked up to him, he said. To Walter, I mean.

Then, He was such a good and steady man. You knew that the moment you met him.

Again, he began. In the battle there was one young soldier got windy. Walter took him in hand. Stay with me, he told him. Go where I go. The soldier followed him after that like a dog.

That'd be like Walter.

Yes.

And what happened to the lad?

That was Luke. He was on the patrol with us.

Explanation enough.

And the other one?

His name was Tommy. Tommy Prosser.

Of course she must know that already, but he had nothing to say about Tommy. So often he had tried to put the thought of Tommy away, as if there had been three of them, not four, as if things could have been different if it had been only the three.

He was a stable lad, from Newmarket, I think. But then she might well know that too.

Not local then. No particular reason for him to join the Norfolks, then.

No, not so far as I knew.

He had said how it had happened, in the letter that he wrote. He had said how they had been ambushed in a clearing, and that it had been very quick – one always said that it was quick, whether or not one knew that it was so. No need to repeat any of that now. Better to say what Walter had said about the orchids.

That touched her. He saw that. She busied herself again to cover the emotion, lifted the pot to pour more tea but the tea was stewed now.

I'll make a fresh pot then, she said.

No, don't worry.

Claire was saying, Really, you're too kind, and besides, we must be getting along.

It was so good of you to come. Stay a little longer, if you can, and the boys'll be back for their dinner.

But we're in your way, Mrs Clarke, Claire was saying.

So they stayed, as they felt obliged to, and drank too much tea.

When the three boys came in they stared at him though they must have been taught not to stare. There was the one who had answered the door to them, who had a cold and had been lying on his bed upstairs, an eight-year-old with a runny nose. He was the middle one. The oldest had a look of Walter, fair and lanky. The youngest was a sturdy little boy with that five-year-old's confidence in being only himself. He would scarcely have known his father.

He stood up when the boys came in and didn't sit again. The tall chair at the table's end should have been Walter's. He kept standing behind it. He said hello to each of them, and they watched wide-eyed. He saw how he mattered to them and felt the weight of it as if he was famous, this famous man who had fought alongside their father.

The atlas was still there on the table. They pulled their chairs close and sat down, and he stood behind them and traced out the journey all over again, for them this time, everywhere their father had been; and still there were names where they weren't needed and no names where they were – and that blank space, of which he could say nothing.

Was it very hot in the jungle, sir?

No, not hot like you'd think.

Somebody must have read them some Kipling. Their jungle was green and hot out of Kipling, with lurking tigers and snakes looped from branches.

Some of the jungle is hot, he said. It was very hot where our army went later, in Burma, but where we were was really quite cold and rainy. It was in the mountains, you see, very high, and there it can be cold, even though it's India. And rainy.

Oh, they said, but he could see that the oldest one – Edward, if he had their names right and this one was Edward – did not quite believe him, so fixed was the place in his imagination. He left it at that. Let them see it as they liked. They did not need to know how dank it was, how clammy in the mist, how the moment you stood still the leeches could swarm at your feet. How they never even came close to a tiger.

When they were finally leaving she said, You must have had a rotten time of it, yourself, in the jungle. I hear you were lost a long time. I'm so glad you made it out.

The house was cold. They lit the fire straight away, took their tea into the sitting room as the fire began to burn. Spent a quiet domestic evening. Supper in the kitchen, back to the sitting room, warm now, listening to the wireless, reading the paper, putting down the paper and watching the fire, and at last, moving to go to bed.

It was good to do that today. Wasn't it, darling?

Yes. He crouched before the fire to damp it down.

She's a nice woman. And they were such nice boys.

She thought how she might one day have boys like that. They would fill the quiet house with noise. They would have big hands and play cricket and grow to tower over her.

I wish I could have done more, he said.

But you did well. You said all she wanted. The boys thought you were a hero.

I'm not.

Not what?

Not a hero.

Will you be seeing the other families? Claire had asked.

No, he had said. No, I don't think so.

So little she knew. So little any of these women knew.

He looked into the fire, crouching, holding the iron poker.

He jabbed at the last log that was burning, turning the log over, bright gobbets falling from it, small yellow flames flaring up, fluid, spilling along its length. He thrust at the log again and saw it break, and there was more fire. He felt the heat of the fire on his face. He could crouch like that for a while, the poker in his hand, seeming ready to spring but holding still. He would stay until the last of it burned away.

Come to bed, she said. It's late.

His hand was tight on the poker. All of him was tight, from his knuckles to his heels as he crouched. He couldn't move. If he moved, he would raise the poker. Stand and lift the poker and smash everything, sweep everything from the mantelpiece, the clock crashing to the floor in tiny parts, hands and cogs rolling, numbers rolling on the Persian rug among the pieces of Ralph's figurines, shepherdesses' heads and white arms and flowered skirts and baskets – but no, they were not Ralph's figurines, they would have been on the mantelpiece before Ralph, on the mantelpiece in the big house where the family had lived before, shepherdesses watching the men who came home so rough from their wars, silently smirking, aware of their reflections in the glass behind them, as Claire's reflection was there now, her face wavering, losing definition – breakable, so easily breakable.

Her voice at his shoulder. Cool as that of a shepherdess.

Come to bed, she said again.

That was why you had to pretend to be a hero, to keep the shepherdesses whole.

She went out then, and when he had looked into the fire for a while longer until almost all colour had died, he put the poker down on its brass rest and stood, his body limp now, and took up the brass fireguard and placed it before the hearth, and turned off the lamps one by one, and closed the door and followed, up the stairs to where she was already in bed. He thought that she was asleep, but she wasn't. He undressed and slipped into the bed in the dark, and she was lying awake waiting for him. She seduced him, gently in the dark, drawing him onto and into her. Her legs and hands clenched him tight and long, taking deep into her every thrust that he made, the dregs of his anger and his semen together.

Then she slept.

He slept for a bit, then woke in a sweat.

Sometimes it was clear in these dreams he had, and sometimes it wasn't, who was who. Two men clasped together. One let go, falling. Or perhaps those specific images belonged not to the dreams themselves but to the moment of waking, to memory not dream. Because the horror was in the waking as much as in the dream, the rational knowledge of what had been done. He knew in his depths that the world had been wronged. That he couldn't put himself right in it any more.

Only if he forgot, could he do that.

Almost always, there was mist in the dreams. Like forgetting, but not forgetting. Sometimes the mist was thick so that he might put out his two hands to touch it, running through. He had to reach out his hands and part it before him and lift it in moist grey swags, only there were more swags beyond, one after another, soft and cold and dewy and heavy and light. The swags fell back behind him soft as curtains, feather-lead weight upon feather-lead weight of mist closing wet and cold on his shoulders and his back, pressing him to run the faster. So fast, he ran. But when at last he ran clear, the fact would still be there, exposed in the light beyond the trees, out there to be seen in the day.

It was becoming day now. The sweat was cold on him, cold on his pillow. Claire still slept. She hadn't woken when he had the dream. That was good. Too often when he had the dreams he disturbed her. What is it, darling, she'd say. And she'd put out an arm across him, move close, but he would lie stiff and retract inside. Let her not know these things. He would lie with open eyes and feel the softness of her beside him and he was not sure whether her presence made it better or worse.

The light seeped in slowly, defining first the rectangles of the windows and then the room itself, until everything in it had depth and form. The wardrobe, the door, the pictures, the chair with his clothes that he'd taken off so carelessly the night before. Claire's dressing table with the mirror above it. Claire herself. The light was enough to see her by now, if not her face then her shape as she slept on, between him and the window from which it came.

He moved to pick himself up, heavy from the night but soft, so as not to wake her.

Go, today, the Viking said

The Viking's English amounted to perhaps twenty words.

Go. Today. Those were two.

He said them that first night in the hut. Good morning, he had said when they met, though it was night. And put out his hand that they might shake. Later he had sat alongside him by the fire, and drank and smoked and said those other two words – Go, today – earnestly as if assured of their meaning, and he had repeated them much later when Charlie stood to go outside, by which time it might indeed have been morning so the words were accurate at last, but Charlie wasn't to know that. Goodnight, was all he replied, with a gesture of his hand, and he went out and walked between the long dark forms of the huts which seemed to sleep beneath their thatch, and there was the whisper of the girl. He lay with her on the platform beneath the overhang of thatch. They lay there for a time warm as animals, and then she rose and went back to her sleeping place in the hut, and he remained until he grew cold, looking out to a bright strip of stars beside the black of the thatch, before he too went in. He cannot have been long in his bed before the Viking came to wake him.

Many of the men were still asleep. The women were up, moving in the grey, stoking fires, bringing water. The girl put out some pans of food on the earth, smiling her newly blackened smile. That morning he noticed her nakedness once more, and marvelled at the ease with which she lived in her skin. She sat on her hunkers and watched while he ate, and the Viking too. Go, today, the Viking said. Again, simply that. This time it made sense.

Goodbye was simple. So simple things were with so few words. The family lined up before the hut, shiny-eyed and smiling, happening to stand tallest to smallest and picturesque as if for some ethnographer's group photo, a couple of small children running along in a blur beside him until they were out of the gate into the breaking mist. The descent from the village was as rapid as the climb had been steep, winding directly down, the mist spinning away from the hills in white strands. He took a last look back when they reached an exposed spur some way off. The sky and the hilltops were clear now. There were figures on the lookout platform waving, knowing that after that spur he would disappear from view.

After that it was only the two of them, but walking all of the day without words as if they each walked alone. They walked down to where the mist still hung, into the damp green depths of a valley so deep and steep and densely grown that after half the day, having crossed the river and climbed upwards again, when they once more reached a point from which he could see out, he saw that he had come only a few hundred yards as a bird would fly it from that open spur. But they would no longer be watching. They would have turned away and gone back to their lives.

Wave, he thought. If only he had some bright banner which he might wave, so that he might draw their attention and they might wave back, and there might be one last contact before he lost them altogether.

Then the trees met once more over the path, and they had to climb steeply again in the trees, up to the height of the village they had left, then down again across another, smaller and roughly cultivated valley, and it was dark by the time they reached the next village where they would spend the night. This new village was a sad straggle of a dozen huts clinging to a narrow crest. They arrived, and the Viking was known there. They were offered food but there was little talk. They slept beside other men on a long bench in a men's house where there were skulls on a shelf at the door. In the daylight next morning there was a crowd gathered to gawp at him when he came out – expressionless, these villagers, he did not know if they were friendly or hostile or just very poor – standing an uneasy few feet back to watch him as he washed, minimally, with a couple of ladlefuls of water, as he ate, adept now at taking food bunched in his fingers. Again, there was the mist breaking, and the children running through it after them as they left – and still he did not know if they might have been hostile and picked up a stone and thrown it – on past the little village's rough defences of stone walls and thorn hedges, running along with them like strangers' dogs as far as some indefinable point in the forest before they turned back, and he went on thinking as he walked, as their shrill voices receded, at what point does a territory end and a dog or a man or a child know that he has become a stranger, where does he know to turn?

So they walked on, away from anyone's territory, through the steep tangle of hills and razorbacks and gorges and valleys. There was no grain to this land, never a long river course or ridge to follow. The Naga god, Hussey would say to him, Hussey who studied and noted everything, the Naga god created this land in a terrible hurry, they believe, because his enemies were approaching, and he had no time to smooth it out. That was how they could stay at war for generations, warring villages separated by their knotted geography but only a few miles apart.

A man, or a dog or a child, instinctively turns where his surroundings become alien, he thought, as the Viking led him on through the alien forest, where the sights and the smells have nothing to do with him any more. His only connection here was to the guide in front of him. Whose silence had become companionship. Whose smell he knew. In whose footsteps he walked.

The Viking's legs were like wood, bone and muscle shaped as if carved out of dark wood by some Gothic carver, but supple and in constant motion, moving before him. He knew the sculpted form of them, the hollow backs to the knees, sinews, calves, the long bare feet grey with old mud. The filthy khaki shorts above them. His eyes fixed on those legs ahead as he tried to keep pace, on those legs and on the ground, and the path they took, step for step. They climbed. The climbs were steep. The pace the Viking set allowed him no energy, no time to look beyond those legs. He could only follow, and see, his mind absent, aware of no more than his walking and his breathing and his sweat. The Viking did not sweat, even beneath the hot helmet. He moved with ease, laying easy sure barefoot steps along the trail, brushing undergrowth lightly aside, moving with a slow rhythm that suggested that he had always strength in reserve. At long intervals he slowed and turned to see if Charlie was still there behind, and Charlie looked up through a mist of exhaustion and met his eyes.

He admired the fine economy in the man. When it was hot in the middle of the day, he carried his red blanket folded over a shoulder. At other times he wrapped it about him with all the style of a Roman senator in a toga. He travelled with few things apart from his clothing: dao, knife and water-gourd, strung from a belt at his waist or in an open-weave cane basket on his back. The only time he removed his helmet was to sleep.

Sometimes there were leeches, though these were fewer since the rains had ended. The Viking flicked them off his bare legs before they took hold. It was automatic to him, to check his legs and his feet and between his toes when they had brushed through wet grasses or stood too long in any one damp place.

There was a fellow who joined them, on the second or the third day, who came out of the forest lightly as a piece of cloud. He could not have said precisely when he had appeared, only that he had suddenly sensed a presence and found the man there beside them. He was young, lithe, light-footed, and wore a black kilt and a necklace of bright beads and tiger's teeth. He spoke a few words to the Viking in whatever dialect they shared and walked with them a while, and when they came to a lush place beside a stream he plucked a head of scarlet poinsettia from a bush that overhung the sparkling water, and put its stem through the hole in the lobe of his ear. But perhaps their pace was too slow for him. As suddenly as he had come, he took off ahead of them and disappeared, away down the path. Fast, light-footed, graceful. A born runner, the thought came to him, like Luke, and he looked to where the man had so swiftly gone and in that instant he saw not that fellow but Luke running back towards him, out of the trees in the mist, a red bloom at the side of his face, and as he saw this his pace did not slow, as he kept pace with the Viking, as here where they were there was no mist, and the green was dense as two walls alongside the path, no space between trees in which to run.

If the sound came, then he would stop. He told himself that. But the sound didn't come. He knew it wouldn't. Luke must be behind many days of walking now. He, Charlie, was walking with the Viking as if he were in a trance.

It was the rhythm and the mindlessness, the constant pace, passing through vegetation which changed but did not change as he climbed and descended, overwhelmingly green and tropical and stifling in the gullies, thinner and darker on the windy heights, the exhaustion as he climbed and descended, his body going on as if it was linked to the Viking's will rather than his own; the combination of these factors that separated him from his body, so that his thoughts moved of their own accord.

Again, Luke behind him, Luke who was afraid in the battle and quiet when he was out of it. Who had volunteered for the patrol probably for no better reason than that Walter had. Luke at the rear where he might have run out of danger. Then Tommy, the sharp sense of Tommy at his back. Luke following Tommy following himself as he followed Walter, as now he followed the Viking. And that other like a shadow between them.

Day after day they went on climbing. Never a piece of flat ground. For hours on end there was only the path and the jungle, never a view beyond, change on the heights and in the valleys no more than change in the density of the vegetation and the weight of the air – sensation, not landscape. Events were no more than the flights of birds. Scarlet bird, lemon-yellow bird. Once a hornbill, flash of pterodactyl beak and black-striped white tail. Look, Luke, look there, that way, there it goes! Then other birds heard but unseen. There was the Nagaland pheasant that didn't chuckle like an English pheasant but only moaned. Listen to that poor bird, Walter had said when he learnt what it was. No sense of humour, d'you hear? And when they finally saw one, Well, what d'you expect? Got no tail on't. Bloody cocks got less tail than hens.

Walter's chuckle then. He looked to see Walter ahead of him again, but there was only the Naga padding on. He missed the heavy tread of Walter's boots and their imprint in the mud.

The pheasant, Walter had said, wasn't an English bird anyway. It had been brought from Asia for the sport. England gave it an easy life, fed it and pampered it and made it stupid, until the guns came out.

It began to rain. The drops on the leaves drowned out Walter's steps. But this was only a shower. The rain before had been elemental, transformative, turning air to water, path to stream. Now there was only this shower, which darkened the sky and then moved on as suddenly as it had come, and left the leaves shining the more greenly and the dark soil steaming. And there was the Viking, walking ahead through the shimmer, passing in and out of pristine beams of light, his horned helmet lit then shadowy among the lace of dripping tree ferns.

Silence. Wet underfoot. The thought of Walter returning. Walter gone to Asia.

A pheasant shot above a Norfolk field, tumbling to the ground. Its wings continue to twitch a last few moments after it lands.

Walter, you damn fool, we should have left, right away. Walked on. Like this man before me, this other long steady man that I follow. What were you thinking, trying to put right what was wrong? Your English decencies don't hold here. You should have known that, after all we had seen. The jungle takes back the dead soon enough, you know that, like any other rotting matter. However many, and whoever they bloody well are: Indian, English, Jap, monkey, all the same.

Or again, Tommy did what he did and we all knew why. Didn't we? Even you knew that. Our chances were better, weren't they, when Tommy had done what he had done?

The Viking knew where to find clean water in hollows and stems. He found fruits they could eat. Wild papayas, which he knocked down from a height with a stick. Limes, astonishingly bitter. Some other citrus, bitter and dry, but the yellow fruits big on the trees like apples in a child's drawing. Beneath one such tree, glistening peacock-blue butterflies, wings wide as his hand. There were more butterflies close to a river, down in the cool of a ravine. They felt the cool of the water coming up to them as they descended. There was a green pool, black shade, hot sand, showers of pale butterflies flying to rocks and opening themselves to the sun. And further up, a series of rapids, and swallows diving low across the water.

The river was high. There was nowhere to cross it, only bamboo posts and trailing vines where a bridge must have been washed away in the rains. They scaled a section of the ravine above the rapids and made their way precariously across rocks with the water swirling beneath them, and once they were across they had to climb higher, the sound of the rapids receding. They came to a belt of pine trees where the ground was bare beneath, and there they rested for a while. He closed his eyes and napped for a moment on the floor of brown pine needles. When he woke he looked across at the Naga in his strange outfit, the baggy shorts and the helmet and the necklace and the ivory bangles, seated with his mahogany legs folded before him and his hands loose on his knees, and saw him anew as he might have seen him once, in some illustration from an adventure story: *Native guide at forest halt*, and he the white explorer. Somehow in all this time he had gradually come to mislay his difference, and now it had come back to him. It was because of the pines. The smell of them had taken him home; the smell and the smooth prickle of the needle floor, and the view between the trees out to blue hills and mounting cloud, which might almost as easily have been in the English north as here. In this moment he was an Englishman again. He felt the disquiet of it.

Up, the Viking said, unfolding himself and taking up his basket. Go. You strong?

Yes.

Strong enough in the body, if not in his wandering mind.

Think nothing. Walk, breathe. Only be. Don't think. Be, like the Naga.

It was a steep climb. The climb was enough. The climb was all. Up through the pines and onto stony upland, slow step after slow step, head throbbing with the altitude. They must be very high. They came at last to a ridge, one of those high razor ridges, and there again the Viking let him rest, though not resting himself now, only waiting, squatting on his hunkers, blanket wrapped around him now because it was windy up there. And when he had his breath back they moved on, following the jagged ridge, the Viking ahead like a prophet with his blanket blown about him. It was hard high walking, but good because they were on top of the whole land. On top of an ocean, it seemed to him. In every direction, as far as his eyes could see, a tossing slate-blue ocean. Only the peaks of the waves did not move. The peaks were frozen as if held in a moment of storm, and it was the cloud that flowed, in the troughs between. And when they came down from the ridge they descended steeply, half scrambling, into a cleft of valley and into the flowing cloud, but within the cloud it was still. He breathed the cool and the damp of it and knew that this valley never could dry out and he had the thought that they would be held there, he and this ancient pacing man, frozen like the mountaintops and like the trees between which they passed, so encrusted with lichen and pendulous mosses that it would seem that the mist had solidified about them.

Now the Viking pressed him on. They still had a way to go.

Another climb. Out of the cloud. Clear sky. Again, a high pass. They crossed a watershed, though he would not know that until later. Nor did he know that they had entered British-administered territory. He would know these things only when he traced the route with Hussey, putting the point of a pencil to a map. The rivers this side of the pass ran to the Brahmaputra, those on the other, to the Chindwin. It must have been here, sir, he would say, this pass. Here on the map. And this must have been the next village where we stopped. Yes, sir, this must have been the way we came. He would soon enough be saying these rational things and marvelling at the clipped sound of his own voice.

In this village, a random sign of civilisation: rice beer, clear and frothy, served to him in a tin mug with chipped white enamel. In the flame-light of the chief's hut, before the central hearth, with the shields and skulls and trophies shadowy on the walls, the white mug offered like a prize.

One day a man turned up and led me away, he had said to Claire. And I followed.

Just like that? she said.

He thought she would have liked to have seen the Viking.

This man who led me out, he said to her, he looked rather distinguished. I wish I had a picture to show you. He wore a headdress with two boar's tusks sticking out of it. I never knew his name. I just called him the Viking to myself because of that headdress.

He heard himself as he spoke, heard his own words, heard how the words reduced the man to an exotic curiosity. A picture wouldn't have helped. He had not begun to mention the ill fit of his shorts or the gaps in his teeth. He did not know how to speak of him, or any of this, and make it true.

He was rather dignified actually, he said then. Rather a good man, and astonishingly at ease in the jungle. He must have had the most amazing sense of direction. He knew the tracks for miles, and when we got out of his area and he had to ask the way, he memorised everything he was told and never seemed to go wrong. It was as if he put together a map in his head. He even spoke a little English, just a smattering, but it was more than almost anyone else knew. The first day or two it was just the two of us, walking on our own, though we stopped at various villages, and then sometimes a man or men from that village came on with us for a stretch, but he was with me all the way.

That's nice, she said. Just like that. Sounds like you were just going for a stroll.

Well, yes, pretty much, he said. His eyes were on hers and his lips didn't quite close on the statement, he looking hopeful like a child who was fibbing and hoped his fib would be accepted. Their eyes exchanged what they both knew: that he wouldn't tell it all and that she would humour him by pretending there was no more to tell, she smiling but her eyes creasing just so little at the corners as if to look into the distance.

Were you sad to leave? I think you were, weren't you?

Well, it had been a kind of haven, I told you that. And I was leaving but I didn't know where I was going, did I? I just knew I had to go sometime, I couldn't stay there for ever.

But you wanted to come home.

There was the war between home and where I was. Though the war wasn't really imaginable any more. Nor was home, for that matter.

Oh.

But I knew the war had to end sometime and that home would still be there.

He didn't mention the dread. He felt it when he drank out of the tin mug. He didn't know how it would be when he was back.

The journey up to that point had been entirely without names. Even when he attempted to trace it, there were no names, no places to be marked on any map. Only ridge, valley, river, village, jungle, mist, sky, day, night, sun, stars, repeating.

———

When he got to Hussey, Hussey would draw a conjectural line. Back in the direction he had noted on his compass, across tangles of contours to the place where his trek might have begun.

What did they call themselves, your tribe?

I don't know.

We should have a name for them. Tell me about them.

With Hussey there would be names. Words, story, a route, flattened onto a map on a plain wooden table. Electric light over the table, so long as the generator kept working, but under the bright light a dimension was lost. There was so much more to all of this than what could be said.

Hussey would take notes, on rough pages, the back of some child's schoolwork, since paper was short in the war.

I think they'd never seen a white man before.

What else?

They were rather fine people. Fine, lively, noble even – not savage once you knew them.

Then we'll call them the Belgae, until we have some better name.

Why's that?

Didn't you read your Caesar? Hussey had read Classics before he joined the Service. He had not lost his academic turn of mind. The evidence of it filled his study which was the one room in the bungalow that seemed truly lived in – too lived in, crammed with ethnographic clutter, headgear and blankets and necklaces and carved wooden skulls still thick with the soot of long-houses, and woven cane belts and penis-guards and a musty stuffed hornbill, piles of papers and books on every surface. Here was Hussey standing on a chair to take down from a high shelf a slim blue volume of *The Gallic Wars*. Translating: *Of all these peoples the most courageous are the Belgae because they are farthest removed from the culture and civilisation of the Province and least often visited by merchants introducing the commodities that make for effeminacy*. Or missionaries, he added. I imagine Caesar would have put them in too, if they'd been about at the time.

I wouldn't have used the word courageous. I don't know if they were courageous.

Well, this is Caesar speaking. He was a soldier after all.

In the nights he would hear Hussey at work. The walls of the bungalow were thin, simple white-painted wooden partitions dividing room from room off the central corridor, the two impersonal front rooms opening onto the veranda, the bedrooms and study at the back. So often in the night, during the weeks that he lingered as Hussey's guest, he would wake in his narrow bed to hear on the other side of the partition the tap of his typewriter or the creak of his movement. Hussey did not seem to sleep much, except for the siesta he took each afternoon, feet up in a planter's chair on the veranda. His face was not the face of a man who slept, papery and drained of vitality, though his eyes were quick. He spent the small hours of the night in ethnography, arranging and typing out whatever notes he had taken in their conversations, whatever contributions Charlie had brought with him to be added to the files of existing knowledge of the Nagas. The days were dedicated to his official work.

He would give Hussey every material detail that he could remember. How they reached the watershed. Every valley and village through which they passed on the way. The rivers they crossed. Whatever encounters they had. One encounter in particular. A cultivated valley, a river, a meeting beside a bridge, and the next climb made in company with four young warriors who wore shorts and carried guns over their shoulders.

What kind of guns? Hussey in his official capacity was concerned about the spread of guns among the tribes.

Old muzzle-loaders, he said, not rifles.

Ah, Hussey said. But perhaps not so old. They make their own, you know, surprisingly skilfully, and fire them with toy caps. I've written to the Governor to ask if we can ban the sale of caps in the markets here. Amazing what little things they pick up from us.

Really, sir? Actually, sir, what I said is not correct, now I think about it. Only two of them carried guns. The other two had crossbows. They wore some pieces of European clothing but all of them had tattoos on their faces and chests.

Where were they going? Were they out hunting?

I don't know. I don't think so, sir. Because they came with us all the way to the beginning of the next village's land, a full day's march, and then they turned back. I think they just came as guides, or perhaps for protection. They came as far as a place where there was a bamboo pole stuck in the ground by the path, and there was a hand strung from it. I saw something a bit like it once before, only it wasn't a human hand that time. When they saw that, they turned double quick and went back, almost running. I think they could have run back in a fraction of the time it had taken us to walk there.

And Hussey would say in his studious way, There will have been some *genna*.

If not a tribal feud then some taboo – some contamination, something forbidden, some line which these other warriors might not cross. Hussey had been observing the tribes and noting their *genna* for a decade.

Genna. It was a foreign word, quite new to him, and yet he thought he could understand it. There were lines drawn in the world. Crossing such a line brought its consequence. Even a civilised man was aware of that sort of thing.

Were you afraid?

Yes, I was afraid. I had thought – it had seemed reasonable to think – that they were taking me to someone like you, to the Army or to some missionaries perhaps, and suddenly there was this grisly hand.

And the man with you?

He just walked on.

He would think, his own line had been crossed already, back there with Tommy and the others. Every tribe has its *genna*.

———

The Viking gave the hand barely a glance. The two of them walked on without so much as a change of pace.

He suddenly feared that they were not making progress at all. They were walking in circles – or if not in circles then in spirals, ascending and descending, scenes repeating. Things seen before would be seen again.

They climbed on steeply, into the territory of whoever had put that sign there. To some other village, some other ridge from which they would again look down on the dark ocean of hills. They would be there by sunset, in a village as well defended as the first he had come to, with stone walls and a gate as great as that other. They would look down as all the sky above turned lilac, and the cloud rolled below as if it would go on for ever, and he would wonder how many other soldiers like himself were circling out there in the mist, how many little bands of warriors, of whatever kind, living and dead.

We're all bloody well the same, Walter, men are all the same, when it comes down to it. We saw that, didn't we?

At the gate a near-naked man crouched with a spear. At his challenge the Viking spoke what he supposed was a name, of someone he knew or to whom he had an introduction. Walter would have been amused to see it. The way he spoke, he might have given his card to the butler of the big house where Walter was keeper. Nakedness didn't make it any less formal. They waited, as callers might at the entrance to the big house, to be invited in.

It looked a powerful village. He could see its strength in the fortifications, and in the way men carried themselves. The head post that stood beside a circle of standing stones at the centre of the village carried clean white skulls alongside the older yellowing ones, and the chief's house to which they were taken was of great length, with a tremendous roof of greyed thatch and gables that soared out over the entrance like the prow of an ark, topped by great carved mithun horns. He knew now that one must enter these long-houses slowly, to allow one's eyes to adjust to the light. It was like entering a tunnel, seeing at first only the pinpoints of light that came through the woven cane walls and the glow of the fire at the centre, and only then the half-lit figures of the handful of men who sat beside it. And to those men one appeared first as a blurred shadow against the light, so that it was a politeness to them also to enter without causing alarm until one's face could be seen. Only then, greetings. And sitting by the hearth, on the hard earth floor or on an ankle-high stool, and taking in two hands the proffered cup of rice beer or bitter tea. Gradually the long room showed itself: great roof posts that seemed to be carved out from whole tree trunks, carved like totem poles with stylised male figures with tall phalluses and flat moon faces; beams carved with heads and tigers and hornbills; actual heads, skulls of men and of mithun, strung along the walls, and shields and weapons, crossbows, spears and daos, and an array of guns.

The chief was a thin old man with narrow hips and a proud chest on which the ribs showed, and a thin pointed face, and such complex tattoos across torso and face that only wide circles were left bare about his eyes, with the effect of making him look, Charlie thought, like a rather regal ant (as he would later say to Hussey, and by the description Hussey would think that he knew the man), and he had acquired a minute pair of shorts, and just a few words of English, but it didn't take many to compliment him on the size of his house, a look of admiration and an expansive gesture of the hands were enough to do that; and he took the compliment and gave Charlie a tour, showing the poles and the carvings and the weaponry, and, wrapping his black-and-white-striped blanket about himself since the air cooled fast in the evening (he, too, knew how to wear a blanket grandly as a toga), taking him out to the bamboo platform at the back of the hut, which cantilevered spectacularly out over a precipice shaggy with jungle, where they watched the sun go down. They stood out there, the old chief like an ancient king, and the Viking and himself, on the flimsy-seeming platform of bamboo, and he looked down and thought of falling. The lilac went from the sky. Mist settled in the rifts between the mountains. The forest canopy directly below grew black – so densely, spongily black, that if he were to step off the edge of the platform, he thought, the fall would be soft, like time. He would be falling a hundred feet through the air and into the softness of the trees, falling slowly, turning over and over, down through the primeval tangle, until he was no more than white bones on the forest floor. He would be like the rest of them, already so many white bones down there. The Viking put a hand to his arm. Perhaps he had swayed forward, just so much. Perhaps they had travelled together so long that the Viking had seen the dream in him. His hand was warm, real. In a moment the swift dusk was gone, and with it, the depths.

When they went back in, the light of the fire was the brighter for the darkness outside.

The chief's great house was packed that night. There might have been a gathering like that every evening, for all he knew, but he doubted it. He suspected that his presence was the draw. So many men flooded in, so many eyes on him at first, men touching him, putting out their fingers just to feel his hair and his white skin, but, as usual in these encounters, his novelty soon wore off. Soon enough he was left in his own silence watching them drink and talk, following none of it, and though he drank also he only fell deeper into his silence. He would not know until he rose how drunk he had become.

He sat, close to the fire and feeling its heat, watching the men talk, bronze faces in the glow, dimmer bodies back from the flame. He watched the bamboo cups passed from man to man, and the pipes, watched the smoke rise to the soot-blackened roof and diffuse along it, seeping out not through any chimney or hole but through the thatch itself, like the house's breath. The underside of the thatch and the roof rafters were encrusted with many years' layers of soot, and anything that had been in the room for any length of time had acquired a blackening of smoke – himself, he thought, included, coughing now and then when the acridity caught the back of his throat, clearing his throat with the cloudy beer for which he had by now acquired a taste.

There was the fire and there were dogs curled close to the fire. That was the best thing to look at, the flames and the glow of embers, and a long silvery dog sleeping beside the chief's gnarled feet. But he was too watchful to rest his eyes in one place for long. There were so many faces. Faces, not masks, though they might have been taken for masks, each one alive with shining eyes beneath its tattoos and its strange and ingenious headdress. Faces framed with necklaces of skulls. Ears stuck with antlers and horns through their hugely extended lobes. Shadows of the horns falling across the faces as they moved. Shadows of the headdresses on the walls. The walls dark – dark umber, but yet not so dark that the heads and the headdresses did not cast shadows there across the arrays of weapons and skulls, a monstrous black dance of shadows as the fire was fed and bright flames leapt up. At moments some movement or shadow or leap of the flames sent a wave of fear running through him. He didn't know if it was because of some difference in this house or tribe, or something in himself. Even the Viking at such moments seemed satanic, with his tusked helmet. He felt the flooding fear, and tried to deal with the fear. He looked back to the silvery dog. Its nose was tucked between its paws. Calm, he told himself, there is no immediate threat here. This is hospitality, not war. Look, these men have almost forgotten your presence. They are like all the others, just drinking and telling stories as men do everywhere when they drink. There is no danger in that. Yet his eyes went on ranging about the room. And then as two men moved and parted, he noticed, squeezed into a space behind them, another figure who sat as still as the dog and himself. He had not noticed him before. He was young, smooth-faced, and he sat cross-legged gazing into the fire. His stillness was arresting, as was his simplicity. He wore only the simplest bead necklaces, no tattoos and no headdress, his black hair in the usual pudding-basin cut. He sat very still and inconspicuous, and yet this separated him from the rest. There was a difference in him, in his posture and in his face, and in his hands, which fidgeted with a twig that he must have picked up from the earth floor, and which did not seem as tough as the hands of a Naga.

Now and then the young man lifted his head a little and his eyes shifted from the fire and cast about, just as his own did, and then for an instant their looks met, and Charlie saw suddenly who, what, he was. And then his head dropped and he was playing with the twig, snapping it into neat little matchsticks in his fingers.

Neither of them moved. Charlie looked, and the Jap looked down. The talk of the Nagas rolled in waves about them, and the shadows moved on the walls, and the fire burned on and a brown hand reached forward to feed a new branch into it, and the silvery dog raised its head at the movement beside it, then settled again. How did a Jap come to be in this village, masquerading as a Naga? Much as he did, he guessed. There would be some story possibly very like his own. Some attack or ambush, some wandering down there beneath the clouds. And here they were – so close, yards apart, each of them in his own terror. They would sit the evening through, not showing themselves or their fear, playing with sticks or swilling rice beer in a tin mug, waiting until the jokes and the stories were done and the Nagas turned in. Then they would lie down to sleep but likely not sleep, yards apart, with the others on the long benches beside the walls, bamboo walls that creaked with the wind or with men's restlessness, and the hearth still red in the centre of the dark room.

All night it seemed he was aware of the room and the walls, the play of shadows that had crossed the walls, the Jap lying there, wondering if the Jap saw what he saw. He was aware that someone had fed the fire with great branches to keep it burning through the night, not looking to see, only glad that the fire was there to warm them against whatever dreams they might have and against the cold mist that seeped through the cracks in the plaited walls. When there was a faint grey light in the cracks he decided that he dared to move. Softly, he rose. He went to the door of the hut but the door was barred. It would have made too much noise to open it, so he crept instead to the far end of the hut and out to the bamboo platform at the back. That creaked too. The floor was made of the same material as the walls, strong broad strips of plaited bamboo that flexed with every movement. There was nothing to see, only air just beginning to be grey, the night almost at an end but the village swathed in cloud. Yet this grey air was cleansing after the oppression of the hut. He could make out the railing at the edge of the platform, black lines in the grey. He took careful steps towards it, one after another, out to where the view would fall if there were a view to be seen.

There, squatting on his hunkers, was the Jap. He had thought it was a dark bundle on the floor, but no, it was the crouching figure of a man, perched right at the edge looking into nothingness. The Jap must have noticed the creak and quiver of the floor, but he showed no sign of it. He might have pushed him then, so easily, he thought, put a hand to his crouched back and rolled him like a ball beneath the rail and out into the cloud. Why would he do that? Because they were enemies. But he didn't. He squatted down a little way off, in much the same position, legs folded, hands dropped between his knees, and watched with him as the grey grew infinitesimally paler. Behind them in the village, dogs barked and cocks crowed. From far below came the waking calls of the unseen jungle.

They crouched there for whatever time it took for light to begin to penetrate the cloud. The air whitened above, and below them a gash broke open so that they looked down suddenly into what seemed to be a swirling vortex, deep and black and plunging to infinity. The sight made him unsteady. He moved his weight, stood, stepped back. The Jap stayed put, balanced on the balls of his feet, faintly rocking. Just a touch, it would take – or the slightest tilt of his own body.

It's all right, he said to the Jap. It's all right. I won't tell. It's okay.

If he didn't get the words, he might understand the tone of them.

And the Jap looked up from the vortex, directly at him, eyes wide in his round, smooth face, which was all the smoother perhaps for the early light which reduced detail and colour, so that it seemed no more than the smooth face of a schoolboy. He didn't know Japs. He knew they didn't grow much in the way of beards. Maybe they always tended to look younger than Europeans. He was sure that this one was anyway younger than he was. He put out his two hands before him, apart and with the palms open in what he thought must be a universal sign that a man holds no weapon and means no harm.

The Jap stood then and stepped close, and bowed to him.

He gave a kind of a bow in return, and the Jap bowed again, lower, so low that he saw the back of his neck, with the Naga hair upon it, but a Jap neck not a Naga neck. He was close enough to know the smell of him. He had the face of a boy but he smelled like a fat old man, of sour sweat and drink or perhaps it was fear seeping through his pores.

The boy turned his eyes away to the horizon.

The sun had yet to rise, but the cloud had pulled back. It was all there to see now, the jungle and the hills, which seemed to go on for ever. It seemed colder in that moment than it had been at any time in the night. He shivered. He didn't want this day to come. He was afraid of it, this day in particular, as this boy beside him was afraid. As if something about it was evil.

The dark of the house and the closeness of the men, which the night before had in themselves been cause for fear, seemed like safety now. As the first streak of yellow appeared on the horizon, he went back in, to his place on the sleeping bench. The space had shrunk, as the Viking had moved in his sleep to fill it. He squeezed in and wrapped himself once again in his blanket, as every man there was wrapped in his blanket. He didn't expect to sleep any more but only to find some warmth. He lay tight in the blanket and looked up to the blackness of the roof, knowing the black softness of the soot, how it coated the cobwebs, how the thatch was stained with years of smoke. How long had that boy been here? Long enough for his hair to grow to a Naga length. Since the battle then. But had he got lost, or had he fled? The latter, by his look. That was what it was that distinguished him most from the Nagas, more than his features or his lack of tattoos, the shame in him. That was it, he saw it now. In all the Nagas, there was pride, more than in any other group of men that he had known. In this man, there was shame.

Would the boy think he was a deserter too? He wouldn't be sure. He was still wearing his uniform, however worn and filthy. God knows, he could perhaps be imagined to be on some Army business. Now he thought about it, he wasn't sure himself. He thought of the others and how he came to be alone, and he thought, well, yes, one might well think that was what he was. Perhaps he also had the look of a deserter, if the boy were to look at him as he looked at the boy. Perhaps it showed, the guilt in him.

The men about him were moving now. He heard someone go to the doorway and pull back the wooden bar that closed it, and saw the sheen of daylight spill along the walls as the doors were pulled open. He turned his head and saw the boy slip out. He must have come back in without his seeing, and been waiting close to the door to make his escape. Maybe he would hide himself until the British soldier was gone. Or he would run into the jungle again, if he had not trusted his words.

He would tell about the Jap later, but it would be a different matter by then.

I think he was a deserter. It's not true, what people say, that Japs never desert. He was very young. Honestly, he looked like a schoolboy. They must have schoolboys fighting for them now.

Speaking with Hussey would be a way of fixing things, extracting them from formless experience and setting shape about them.

The Nagas had dressed him up as one of them, he would say. Undressed, rather. He was almost naked – just a kilt about his hips, and necklaces and armlets, his hair grown out and left long at the top and shaved at the sides. Knowing them, they probably had fun doing it. I think they might have done it to me if there'd been half a chance of making a fair-haired Englishman look like a Naga.

No, he wouldn't have made a good Naga. Nor would Hussey – the two of them pale, knobbly, English. Give them painted tattoos and headdresses and spears, and they might be comically dressed for the Governor's fancy-dress ball at Shillong. It was strange to be speaking with an Englishman again, the words spilling out before him, heard and understood, and spilling on, with all their implications. How absurd the thought of a Naga would seem to everyone at the ball. But not here. Hussey knew that. There was nothing funny about them here, nothing the slightest bit funny.

Coming to Hussey he would see his own world again, but turned about, so that every familiar piece in it would be strange to him. There would be the initial shock of the half-timbered bungalow, with the hedges and the flowerbeds, like a lodge you might find beside the gates to some country house, in the Lakes or in Wales, somewhere where trees hung damp and whitewash swiftly greyed. Then the man in the long cane chair, unravelling his outstretched legs and standing as they approached, putting down his pipe and walking to the top of the steps.

Good Lord! A clear English voice. A man with the look of a schoolmaster, bony face, light blue eyes, thinning sandy hair; his voice one that has learned an authority that has not come to it naturally, as if from the habit of speaking to boys and across a classroom or an assembly hall. Hello, and where have you come from?

And he would stutter. The words failed in his throat. He was Lieutenant Charles Ashe, that was who he was; and he couldn't say where he'd come from but only wave a trembling hand towards the hills and the clouds.

Come on up, my boy, sit yourself down. Hussey guided him up the steps to the veranda as a master might have guided him into his study, indicating a seat. But before joining him he called a servant to bring some refreshment to the two Nagas who'd brought him, the Viking who stood at the foot of the steps, ill at ease, and the other who squatted so confidently beside the marigolds with his basket on his back.

He would be barely able to speak, that first day. He would have his bath, his familiar unimaginable hot bath, and after that he would let Hussey do the talking. He would not begin his story until the next morning, by which time the man would be all of a night's march away, and free of his load.

He would see that Hussey had already been up for hours. No doubt things had been dealt with and reports had been written, but Hussey had waited for him before sitting down to his daily boiled eggs and tea and toast and marmalade. When they had finished and the servant had cleared the things away Hussey did not move but stayed where he was sitting, lit his pipe, looked to him, expectant. He would turn his chair then, just slightly so that he could look away from his listener to the hills and the clouds that poured across them. And he would begin. Sometimes he would raise his legs and put his feet to the latticed wooden veranda rail and gaze out there, sometimes pull them tight beneath the chair and put his head to his hands. He would tell the story of the Jap first. That was as much as he could deal with now. One thing at a time.

I wouldn't have told, you know. I'd have let him be. He could have lived through all of the rest of the war out there and no one would have known. He could have lived there for ever if he liked.

———

They waited on a wide dark wood bench beneath the porch of the chief's hut, where the roof reared up above the carved pillars. The mist had quite gone. The sky was blue and the low morning sunlight penetrated almost to the back of the porch. There should have been nothing to menace him any more, not in the crude carvings nor in the circle of tall grey stones set in the bare mud before the house and the head post with its bizarre trophies, strung through the nose sockets, looking now squalid and paltry beneath the directness of the light. These things were nothing to do with him, with his culture or time. They would soon be the past, and he would move on into the present which was where he belonged – and sometime not too far off, whenever the war was over, the present must surely come here also, and these things would be buried and gone, so that there would be only the stones standing and the memory, and grass growing about them and they tilting as the ground in which they stood subsided. It was morning. The sun was getting warm and he was ready to leave. He shifted position and took out his watch. He had got into the habit of keeping the watch deep in his trouser pocket. On his wrist it attracted too much attention from the Nagas and he had feared he might lose it to one of them. The time it told wasn't necessarily correct – there had been days in these months when he had failed or simply ceased to wind it, and whenever he had set it again he had done so by guesswork around sunrise. But whatever the hour it told, it reckoned the passage of time as well as it had ever done, and it had that way that watches have of slowing the minutes the more you looked at it.

The Viking sat out the wait with his Gothic patience. Time didn't seem to matter to the Viking, or to anyone there as much as himself – except for that Jap. It would matter to him. That boy must have been desperate for him to be gone, as soon and as far away as he could go. He wondered where he had got to, if he was hiding in some other hut in the village, watching as he did the minutes pass, or out in the jungle where time like air so swiftly became dense and ancient. He felt the kinship between them. What would he have done if the situation had been reversed? He would have longed to be alone again with the Nagas, for safety, and for anonymity: no one there would see into him and know what he was. Because the Jap must have seen into him as he thought he had seen into the Jap; as the Viking could never do, for all their familiarity, because the Viking lived in a different time.

A thin ginger cat arched its back and rubbed past his leg. He put out a hand to stroke it but it recoiled. Again, he looked at his watch, and to the Viking who sat so still.

He dropped his hand once more in invitation, and slowly the cat came forward to it. He could feel the ribs beneath its fur, the purr which like the watch stretched out the seconds.

The cat was gone soon as the other man came. He came fast, firmly towards them, slightly bow-legged, a short stocky man with a blanket over his shoulder and a basket on his back, and the cat slipped away.

The man had a bold swirling pattern of tattoos on his face and he wore tusks in his ears, and no hat but a thick mop of very black hair, and a necklace of five brass heads, and broad white ivory arm and leg rings that accentuated the muscularity of his limbs. Charlie had noticed him the night before, close to the fire in the hut, a bold fellow but one who didn't stare, as if he had known already what British people were. A tough one, he thought. Built like a rugger player, a good man for a scrum, with sloping shoulders and a thick neck and a head like a nut. He saw how athletic the man was as they left the village, at the threshold stone beyond the gate, where he made a sudden vertical bound, knees folded up, arms spread wide, and flew in the air. He didn't know then that it was a leap from a Naga dance, that this man was an admired dancer. He wouldn't know anything about the dancing until he was with Hussey, but the single move was stunning. He caught the elation of it, some brimming excitement in the man, and almost the man danced again as he sauntered ahead of them down the first steep descent, down steps and slopes and loops, down into the gorge he had seen from the bamboo platform – and after all that wait it was an exhilarating plunge into the early morning's vortex – that was so lush and green now that the mist was gone. Once they paused – it was rare that the scrum-half paused – and he felt his head throb with the beauty of it, as they climbed a rock that looked out over the gorge. They were so much lower here that the air was already dense and hot. The jungle sounds were close beneath. They could hear the hidden river and the distant roar of the waterfall that fed it, and turning to look upstream he saw the white thread falling hundreds of feet down the cliff.

That first stretch, he will remember, was the most beautiful stretch that he walked in all of that trek. There was the waterfall so luminous in the sunlight. A hint of rainbow in the air above it. The tangle of the vegetation that encrusted the cliff. The eagles that hung in the sky. The lightness in him, at being released from the village and the thought of the Jap – so swiftly he had forgotten that Japanese boy – and at the pace which the scrum-half had set, slaloming downhill. When they came lower and entered the jungle it was the sort of jungle he would one day wish that he could describe to Claire, if he could ever describe to Claire anything of those next two days: the green dusk, the bronze of the earth floor, the orchids which grew thick on these trees, the cool rush of the river when they came to the foot of the torrent and found a bridge. And after they had crossed they rested on long smooth rocks. The scrum-half put down his basket before him and smiled, some heavy package in it the size of a football wrapped round with a cloth, visible through the openwork of the weave. When the scrum-half smiled the lines of his tattoos distorted his face into a clown's. He smiled broadly and put his strong hand to Charlie's arm and spoke: You British, give me medal.

Maybe, Charlie said, wondering if he'd wear it beside the five brass heads on his chest. Not mentioning that the feat of bringing him in would hardly be considered such as to merit a medal.

Then the man stood, and swung his basket onto his back, shedding a cloud of flies that had fastened to the cloth-covered bundle.

Suddenly Charlie understood.

Beyond the river they walked through a thicket of bright green reeds tall above their heads. The path between them was tight. The scrum-half led. The Viking came at the rear. They walked close there and in single file. Then they were back in the forest but the path widened, and he could fall back and walk beside his guide. All he could know was what he read in the Viking's eyes. He saw that the Viking also knew. He must have known it even when they were waiting that morning. And he saw that they must keep with this man. The thing in the basket and the medal were their insurance that they would get to where they were going. They walked under a bower of wild wisteria, the sweet scent all about them.

———

On the last climb before Mokokchung it came on very hot. Sweat poured off him. The jungle sound amplified in his ears. The figure of the scrum-half drove on ahead, grotesque and relentless.

Rain, the Viking said.

How, rain, when it was so hot?

Within minutes the shower came and pelted down, and went, and took the tension from the air and left it clean.

Mokokchung looked new-washed when he first saw it, the town spilling down the green hills, roof tiles and thatch shining, the white mission church like absolution.

There was the bungalow, black and white, the orange flowers before it, the Englishman on the veranda with his legs loosely crossed on the long arms of the chair.

Homecoming. The Englishman putting his feet to the floor, rising, putting out a hand. The feel of the cool English hand shaking his, a freckled bony hand in his own sweating one. His beige cotton shirt. The smell of his pipe. Suddenly he and the Englishman were up on the veranda and there was a gulf between them and the two Nagas, one of them shy and the other bold; the Viking shifting from one foot to the other at the base of the steps, and the scrum-half squatting behind his basket like a trader with something sought-after to sell.

Handshake. Name. Regiment. Story – no, that too complicated. Leave the story for later. Take a bath. This kind man with the cool hand offered him tea, and after tea, a bath, and a servant to run the bath for him, and to bring him towels, many-times-washed no-longer-white towels, and then he was alone, and he washed each piece of himself and lay back in the bath and saw his body from that angle, so slightly distorted, and wondered at its being his, the sunburnt bits and the pale bits, the bony knees, the filthy toes which would need to be scrubbed some more and have the nails trimmed, the hands likewise, the slack penis nudged by the movement of his hand in the water. (And even when he has come home, again and again, there will be moments of such strangeness, as if the homecoming will never be completed. Again, when he is really at home, coming in from the farm – and there is no work more physically connected to the place that is home than the work of the farm – he will go upstairs and run hot water loud into the cast-iron bath, and step in with the water still running, and when the bath is full he will reach to turn off the taps, and regard himself again as a stranger, lifting the soap from the wooden bath rack, standing to wash, seeing himself in the long mirror above the basin.)

Clean then. Beard not shaven yet – let that wait for the barber tomorrow. A glass of whisky put in his hand, and the kind man offered a cigarette.

———

In Mokokchung there were words. For the unspeakable as well as all the other things. For what was in the basket as for the flowers beneath which they had walked.
Head.
Jap's head.
Beheaded.
Wisteria.

Hussey had books in which he might find the descriptions and the names of the flowers and the plants and birds he had seen, some of them having names in both English and Latin, and those that did not yet but would soon enough be given botanical names having them in one or other of the Naga dialects, or already a variety of names in different dialects which Hussey had noted down.

He sat with Hussey in the bungalow, that first evening, when he had bathed, the servant closing doors and windows and lighting the coals in the narrow fireplace since the nights so quickly grew cool, and tried to find the names for things. He felt marvellously clean and held a tumbler of Scottish whisky in his hand. That had a name: Glenfiddich. Supplies of whisky were short because of the war. Hussey had been saving the bottle for visitors and enjoyed the opportunity to pour a second glass.

Damn fellow wanted a medal, Hussey said. I sent him packing.

He's gone then, he thought. He had no reply. He took a sip of the whisky, looked about the room, at the muted prints on the walls of Indian palaces and temples, which might have been Hussey's or might have been inherited from a predecessor, at the faded backs of books which he assumed were Hussey's own. So he need never see that man again.

Well, what would you have done? Hussey asked of his silence.

I don't know.

Would you say he committed a crime?

Of course it was a crime. It was murder.

Hussey looked tired, muted and foxed like the prints.

There's a war going on.

He had been without words and now the words he heard confused him. These Nagas were headhunters, after all. That was what people called them. That man was a Naga. He is a headhunter, and we are fighting a war. So where does the crime begin?

It's a muddle, Hussey said. It's a bloody muddle, all of it.

He put a hand to his brow. It was pale for the hand of a man who had spent thirty years in the East, but spotted and freckled.

How can they hope to get it straight when we bring them this muddle? We tried to stop it. At the start of the war here, we told them not to take Japanese heads. How are they to understand our rules?

What did you do with him?

I told you, I sent him packing.

No. I mean the Jap.

Best to have the thing buried.

Where?

In the cemetery.

Hussey digressed then, moving the subject tactfully elsewhere. He sensed that Hussey must be a tactful man.

The Angami Nagas, Hussey was saying, in the voice of the ethnographer he liked to be when he was not being a colonial official, a musing thread of a voice which seemed somehow more natural to him. You will have seen some of the Angami, of course, they will have been the first you met when you came to the country, they live in the area about Kohima, we've known the Angami for longer and know rather more about them than we know about other tribes, and they're educated now too, you know, and Christians, since the missionaries have been with them for years, and their lives are changing so it's worth making the effort to record what we can of the old beliefs before they disappear – well, the Angami, and very likely other tribes too, I should think, have rather a nice custom that if a man dies away from home, a lock of his hair is brought back and attached to a wooden image that is substituted for his body at a funeral ceremony. I've read that the Japanese do something similar. It need be no more than a few strands of hair or a nail clipping, but it's taken home so that the family can commemorate the dead, each year on the day when they celebrate their ancestors. The basis is in ancestor worship, of course. I think you will find variants of this custom throughout Asia.

Is it done? he blurted out, interrupting and rising unsteadily. Is it buried already?

I should hope so. Not a thing you want to keep hanging around.

No, of course not. It's good that it's buried. Otherwise—

He went out, leaving Hussey by the fire. He walked to the edge of the veranda and stood looking into the dark. Where the sun would rise in the morning, that way was Japan. As if, otherwise, he must take it there, or some hairs of it at least, soon as the war was over.

Plough

She caught him staring, as if she didn't exist. As if she might pass her hand before his eyes and he wouldn't so much as blink. Not even the shadow of her hand might touch him, or the air displaced by its passing.

He was so much there, so physically there in the room, but unblinking, unseeing.

She had curled her hair and dressed for him but he didn't see it. Before she came downstairs she had sat and put on her woman's face before the mirror with the window and the flat land and the outlines of the bare trees outside. As if lipstick made her more visible.

Did you hear the weather forecast? she said.

Weather should matter to him. After all, it was weather that shaped his days.

They say there's a blizzard on the way. They say there's a cold winter ahead.

What's that?

He was too far away even for weather.

They say it'll be a cold winter.

Ah, is that so? Not good then, if they're right. Better get going and do all we can before the blizzards arrive.

He left his cup on the table and went down the passage and took his big coat from the hook by the door, and his scarf and gloves and cap from the shelf above it, and put on his boots and went out.

He was out all morning. He came in briefly for lunch then wrapped up and went out again, as the clouds began to weigh in the sky.

She took Jess out and saw the clouds, saw that the forecast was accurate, that the snow would be with them soon. She could hear his tractor across the fields tearing up the ground.

He saw her walking there, saw the dog and the clouds. Only the clouds mattered. In whatever time remained before the snow came, all that mattered was the work – the doing of it, the concentration, the steadiness, the looking ahead along the line, the looking back to see the soil thrown up slick and chocolate-dark where his blades had gone, the slow pulling of twenty-odd horsepower through the earth. But it was cold. The cold got to him as the hours passed and the weather moved in. He grew numb, as if he was only a part of the groaning machine. There was a precision to this work that he was still learning, that made it a good thing to do. He needed to align the furrows precisely for each stetch that he ploughed, turn the tractor along the headland, align again for the return. At each headland he held still a moment, while the throb of the engine continued and the smoke of the exhaust rose before him, the smell of it in his nostrils as it had been all of the day.

There are moments when the world changes shape, distorts, blackens. When the shape into which it turns seems so complete and so entirely credible that you are convinced by it even though you know that the appearance is temporary and will pass. So he set out the next furrows, ploughing into the dark earth as the snow began to fall.

It came in fine flakes at first, out of the bruised sky. The flakes melted soon as they touched the earth, making it blacker, not white. The trees stood out more black than ever above the hedges, the taller elms like crooked fingers, that had been planted to give him the lines to which he must work. The snow thickened. He reached the headland again. Drove the tractor along to the next pointing finger, churning the soil as the snow fell to heal it. One last time across the field, he told himself, then home to the yard. The flakes had become icy chips, swirling about the bare trees. There was no sky now, no land, but only the snow. A piece of him wanted to keep on at the work, as if there was no other choice but to remain. If he were to go on, the flakes would pare him away, his face, his skin, down to metal and bone.

———

Darling, you look so cold.

He went straight to his study, closing the door.

Why don't you come in the kitchen where it's warm?

No, it's fine. Won't be here long.

Let her go, he thought. Let her not fuss.

———

He stared at his hands on the desk. Numb hands, frozen fingertips, reddened knuckles, slowly warming as he flexed them. Then he lifted his head. He looked all round the room. It was his room but not his room. All these things in it, so many of the things in it, not only the furniture but the lamp, the blotter, the pen stand, the paper knife, these things were Uncle Ralph's. The ugly bulbous glass ashtray that Mrs T had emptied that morning. So many of the papers even, in drawers and on shelves in piles and in boxes, Ralph's. And the books on the shelves were his and Ralph's mixed together, books on country pursuits and military history, old leather-bound volumes of Gibbon and Shakespeare and Dickens, and the heroic stories he used to read when he was a boy, Orczy and Dumas and Buchan, and *King Solomon's Mines* and *The Prisoner of Zenda*.

He took up a packet of cigarettes from the desk, lit one, dropped the match in the clean ashtray. The picture above the fireplace had been Ralph's. A landscape – or perhaps you called it a seascape – pale dunes tufted with grass and waves breaking before them. It was by someone good, Ralph had told him, though he had forgotten the painter's name. There were Ralph's guns in the cubby-hole in the corner that Ralph had called his gun room; Ralph's treasured Purdey, which he hardly ever used, which was perhaps the most valuable thing there, a fine shotgun from the most famous gunmaker in Mayfair, the sort of gun that merited a room to itself. He was tempted to take it out, if only to hold it. He had handled it enough to know the sure feel of it, its weight, the polished wood of the stock, bespoke for Ralph, the engraved metal of the trigger-guard, the dense leafy pattern scrolling about his initials. He would put his touch where Ralph's had been.

He felt his uncle at his shoulder now, the tobacco-and-tweed smell of him. Time, Ralph would say, it takes time. Patience, boy. Ralph had taught him to shoot, in the winter holidays when he came to visit. Ralph stood beside him in the field as the pheasants were driven towards them. Wait. Don't fire too soon. Pick out your bird and watch it, and let it pass overhead. There's more of a target then. One bird separated from the others, one black cross against the sky. Stock against his shoulder, hand steadying the barrel, finger poised.

It was dark outside the window, the curtains not drawn. It was so dark that you couldn't see the snow but only the reflection of the room and the man at the desk. A reflection that was not Ralph, but some other gentleman farmer come home from war. Was that him? Was that him, here, at this other man's desk?

Claire came in with tea on a tray.

Really you should light the fire, it's so cold in here.

She went to draw the curtains and the reflection was gone.

Would Ralph have understood about the *genna*? If he did understand he wouldn't have spoken about it. Men like him didn't have words for things like that. Only a shrug, a set of the mouth, a turning away to some practical matter.

———

If you hold too long and don't shoot, the bird will pass. You hold your gun and watch it glide on without another beat of its wings, like a paper dart released and flying straight, losing height so gradually that you barely notice it drop, gliding where it is aimed towards the dark far trees where no guns are.

His body was cold, coming beneath the sheet, letting in a slice of cold air.

They had been warm by the fire, in the sitting room after supper, he with his book lying open on the arm of his chair, eyes closed, mouth a little open. Dozing after a long day out in the field. She nudged him gently but he moved with a jolt and the book slipped to the floor. She said she'd put a hot-water bottle in the bed. He should go up. She'd just take the dog out first.

No, I'll go. I'll take Jess. I think I left a barn door open.

He spoke with urgency, though she couldn't see the cause for it.

Anyway, he said, I'd like to see how much snow there's been.

What had it mattered? Snow was snow. And however much snow was there now, that was not the snow that they would find in the morning. There was all of a night between then and morning.

Now his body was cold, closing on hers to borrow her warmth. You asleep?

I was waiting for you. What were you doing, all that time?

She shuddered at his icy fingers, pushed them back against his body, took her own warm hands to him instead. As they made love she pulled the sheet and the heavy blankets over them into a cave, holding the warmth they made about them, holding tight, not letting it out, not letting the cold get in.

Then he was really asleep, a weight on her. She must shift his body away, pull back her arm that lay beneath his shoulder. Whatever he had brought to her, she could not rid herself of it: the cold, the black-and-whiteness of the night. She curled up, away from him, hands to her naked belly and between her legs. She wondered if she would know, if she were to conceive. If a child might be conceived in such cold. How such a child would be. She lay awake until the wind dropped and the blizzard seemed to have passed. If it was still snowing, the snow would lie smooth now. Even so, she barely slept. Soon as there was light she got up and looked out, and went outside.

He had a gun in his hand. Only it was just a toy gun, a little weightless thing that fired caps – snap, snap, snap, and the smell of gunpowder. Hussey was there, and the Governor from Shillong. He didn't run this time. He shot into the mist, and where he shot holes opened, and vapour puffed out through the bullet holes like men's warm breath when they stand out in the cold. They're only percussion caps, the Governor said. He's not doing any harm.

———

The room was strangely white when he woke, that bareness to it that comes when light reflects off snow. Her pillow was cold and the curtain at one of the windows was half drawn. He saw how she had been awake early, and drawn back the curtain to look out, as he did now. There were her tracks in the snow, running from the front door – she had gone out from the front, unbolting the big black front door that they so rarely used so that she could make her path directly out across the centre of the whiteness – a bold straight path like some determination in her that led, he could see now, to her bundled black figure out there before the trees. The path made it hers, all that ground hers, she the first to tread the snow. As he watched, she turned and took a careful look back across the garden towards the house, and for a moment stretched out her arms with raised beckoning fingers, like a distant conductor calling her orchestra in, calling the instruments to order, then slowly let them drop, and spun round, and went on. He stood before the cold glass of the window and watched as she did that and then walked away through the trees out of sight, and he stayed there growing colder when there was no one to see, no movement anywhere, but only the snow and the dull white sky. He looked out to the fields. You could not tell any more what was grass and what was stubble and what was plough. No harm. All that dark earth he had ploughed had been covered over.

———

You should go out, she said when finally he came downstairs. It's lovely out there.

The light glowed over the yellow tablecloth. She was cooking breakfast. She had put out a jug of coffee already.

I saw you.

I saw you too, at the window. I waved. I thought you might come and join me.

So was it for him that she had held out her arms? She had seemed too far off.

You looked strange standing there, she said. Like a ghost.

She laughed. She was elated, cleansed of the night by the snow.

Whose ghost? he said. And she said, I don't know, darling, just a ghost, any ghost.

When breakfast was over they went out together, with Jess, out from the back door this time and through the yard, and walked the farm. Perhaps it does not matter so much to the land, he thought, what men do on it. It is only to men that it matters. The land will always be there. Tear at the surface, blast it with craters, and soon enough, it covers over. These fields of his have become white in a night. The plough wasn't smooth, not quite. Clods of soil broke through on the ridges and the deep snow of the furrows was purpled with shadow. But the rest of the land was smooth. The distance seemed smooth and flat and unmarked right to the horizon.

There was that early cold spell, and then a time of mild-
ness, and then cold again. The first winter they spent on the
farm would be the coldest in memory. At least Charlie had
those difficult fields done, the headlands finished off late in
December when the land was crisp with frost. Billy said they
were well on. If Billy said that then it was probably true. Billy
knew this farm better than anyone. Got those fields down at
least, though we'll have our work cut out when this freeze is
over. Mind you, back when I started, with the horses 'n all,
it all took a good while longer. Oh really, she said, learning
things that she hadn't thought needed knowing. And how
many horses did you use? And how long did it take? It didn't
take much to set Billy talking. Billy's talk ran back so far. Fifty
years' work on this one patch of land, more if you counted the
days he had come out as a boy picking stones. Billy belonged.
When she had Billy there, she too had a sense of belonging, or
knew at least what belonging meant.

Hard weather, but there's something in it. A good freeze'll
kill off the pests. Forecasters say we're in for a big one. P'raps
we're needing it, after what's gone on, the war I mean, all
that's gone on.

At the end of January, when they had just thought they
might be through, came the worst blizzards, and on into

February and March. For those months she looked out onto a flat world almost without colour. From the kitchen, a view of a frozen yard, glassy with ice and then deep in snow, a path cleared across the cobbles, dirtied heaps up against the walls; and from the long windows at the front of the house, drifts now across the fields, a whiteness that ran to a sky which was close to white in itself.

She liked having Billy in because he broke the silence. It was so quiet, otherwise. The snow seemed to muffle even the radio waves, the voices on the wireless crackling and fading as she went across to turn the volume up.

Sometimes he brought in a piece of game, a couple of pigeons or a rabbit or a partridge. He taught her how to deal with them, his old hands gentle with the dead things, deftly skinning or plucking – a drop of spit on blunt thumbs helped the grip on downy breast feathers – how to open a bird's crop to see what scraps of green or seeds or berries it had found to eat, how to pull pink and blue and burgundy entrails out into a bowl.

There you are, madam, that's right. We'll have you a country woman yet.

Not quite yet. The smell of the bird clung to her fingers even when she had scrubbed them. She rubbed a scented cream into her skin and inspected her painted nails.

When Charlie came in, there was the little partridge plucked and drawn and trussed, neat and blood-dark on a white plate. Good old Billy, he's brought us something today, has he? I meant to go myself. Too late now, it'll be dark soon. Perhaps I'll go tomorrow. Yes, she'd say. You should do that. She looked at him standing there, hands idle at his sides. The snow seemed to have stilled him within the house, in his study where he lit his own small fire, after the Aga had been stoked in the morning, where he had his own warmth and his own thoughts, whatever they were, and sat at the desk and rested his head in those empty hands. There were only two rooms now that they heated in the day, his study and her kitchen, where he came to eat or just passed through on his way outdoors, passed through as briefly as he passed through the cold spaces in the house, and didn't stay, where he didn't stop for her company, though she had it so warm. Yet his presence was there, all the time. She couldn't escape it. She'd see the closed door of the study and want to hammer on the wood. She hated whatever it was that he did there, his paperwork or his brooding. If he would not be with her, then better that he was outside. Hunting. Wasn't that what men were supposed to do? Wasn't that in them, deep?

Finally the mood took him, and he put on his heavy coat and hat and boots, and took his gun and called Jess to him and went out, and now she was jealous that he had broken out. Let him freeze, she thought. She heard isolated shots. Let him miss, let the birds get away. She pictured the black wings of birds scattering in a darkening sky, others thrown up from trees in which they had already settled. The shots sounded far off, deadened in the snow. Then there was silence, and for a moment she was afraid. Let him come back, she thought then; and then he did come back, and he had two pigeons in his hands and he looked the warmer for having been out in the cold.

———

Do you think the Nagas know boredom? he said.

He spoke as if boredom hurt. As if each day hurt in this snow-bound house, all these days that were all the same, the two of them criss-crossing from room to room, he to his study – but it was still Ralph's study, wasn't it, though he had begun to move things, to sort the papers, put some for burning – she to the kitchen. She had papers too, white paper spread on the kitchen table like the snow, which had to be moved aside when they sat down to eat. She was making a plan for the garden, but she knew nothing of gardens, only what was in Ralph's old books, and already there was a smear of marmalade on the paper, the ring of a teacup. Later she brought the books with her into the sitting room. They lit the fire there just for the evenings. It didn't seem necessary as they already had two rooms warm. It was a waste, really, to heat another whole room and sit in it and say so little, and do only the same things that they had done in those other rooms in the day. A waste of wood, all for some kind of custom that they seemed to think it was necessary to keep.

It was you who lived with the Nagas, not me.

I don't think they did. They didn't know boredom and they didn't know time. They just lived.

Then shall we stop winding the clocks? This clock, and all the other clocks in the house? None of them are right anyway, they all chime at different times. Then there won't be any time here.

There'll still be the clock on the church.

Yes, but you hardly hear that. When the wind's in some directions, you don't hear it at all.

At that moment, just as she said that, the power went again. He took up a box of matches in the flicker of the firelight, and lit the candles, and their light doubled in the mantel mirror, a golden glow on the clock and the figurines and on the reflection of the room. Then he went to the chair where she sat and pulled her from it to the rug before the fire.

No sense of time now. Only the fire burned and the clock ticked on. But the pressure of time within her, an urgency in her for the future. The need to take him in to the dark core of her and make a child.

He saw the man across the marketplace. A small man, quick-moving. It was the way the man moved that first drew his attention. A little bit bow-legged. Bundled up in a tweed coat with a peaked cap and a bit of ginger hair showing but a thick wool scarf and the collar of the coat pulled up obscuring part of his face. He knew that ginger hair, and the way the man moved. A jockey. A Newmarket man. What was he doing in Swaffham? But there was no racing this winter. They wouldn't even be riding out. There was snow, and the going frozen beneath. The horses would be in the stables – and the jockeys, the jockeys might as well be in Swaffham as anywhere. The man came out of the bank, put his hands in his pockets, walked along swiftly, shoulders hunched, walking towards them down the length of the marketplace, past the parked cars, and the dainty market building that was like a temple, and the few stalls that braved the winter.

What is it, darling?

They had just got out of the car. They came into town together when there was shopping to do so that he could be there if the road was blocked or the car got stuck, and anyway Claire didn't like to drive in the snow. Now she had taken the basket out from the boot of the car but he was still standing with his hand to the driver's door, transfixed.

Who is it, someone you know?

The man was coming closer. He would walk right by them. His hands were in his pockets and his head was bent down into his scarf and his collar. He might have been Tommy's brother. Did Tommy have a brother? Might almost have been Tommy.

No, he said. It's nothing. Nothing at all. He found that he had slipped the car keys into his pocket. He had to take them out again to lock the car door.

He knew that he would go on seeing them. All the rest of his life he will be catching sight of them, their heads, their backs, their gestures on the street.

He didn't run after them any more. There had been that time when he and Claire were just married. They had been away on honeymoon and had just got off the train at Euston, he carrying the suitcases, Claire walking beside him to the taxi rank. He had dropped the cases even as he ran. Then come back to her standing beside the cases looking shocked.

She had said the same thing.

Who was it, darling? Was it someone you knew?

No.

Just someone who had the look of someone that he had known.

Nothing. No one he knew. Every time he said those things he felt a little further from her. There was glass between them. Cold glass, like ice and like mirror. He had had the sense before, when he came down from the hills to Calcutta, and on the ship, most of all on the ship home, but even, now he thought about it, on that first arrival in Mokokchung, on seeing Hussey and his bungalow and all that was so familiar. He had thought that it would leave him, the sense that this world he had come back to was a looking-glass world, not quite the world that he had left but one turned about, reversed, left to right and right to left, changed in surface if not in substance – or was it in substance but not surface? – just so much distorted. There had been stretches of time since he had come to the farm when the feeling quite left him, but at other times it persisted, as now in this winter in the snow, when there was nothing he could do to occupy himself, the physical world about him covered over and gone to ice. Now in Swaffham this man walked past, head down into his scarf, blowing or whistling oh-so-softly, the breath coming like steam from between his lips. He was very like Tommy, even in his features. But not Tommy. And besides, there was a sheet of glass between them also. The glass was between him and everyone. He wanted to break the glass, but glass when it broke was sharp. What is it, darling? she asked. He did not want to hurt her.

Only he did hurt her.

Don't you trust me?

He was driving the Hillman, slow in the slush. The main road had been cleared and gritted. All that way she had been silent. There had been only the sound of the car and the snowy landscape that was beginning to darken, and the almost empty road. Now they had turned off on a by-road towards the village. One of the other farmers had come through with a digger and pushed the snow from the centre of the road, leaving it high at the sides. There was just one pair of tracks to follow. If they met another car someone would have to find a place to reverse to get past.

Of course I trust you.

Then why do you tell me lies?

What do you mean? he said, but only automatically. He needed his concentration for the road. The slush that had been worn down during the day was beginning to freeze once more.

You knew that man. Who was he?

No I didn't. I just thought I did. For a moment.

A rather long moment.

No, really, I was thinking about – I don't know what.

Why not say so, if you thought he was someone you knew?

Darling, I'm trying to drive.

But she didn't let it go. He took a glance at her and saw that she was crying. Why cry now? Why cry in the car in the snow? Why, when he was driving and they were in the car where words echoed back and couldn't escape? Hard enough to drive as it was, and now there were ribbons of fog drifting towards them, caught in the beams of the head-lamps. She didn't let it go at all. She went on speaking as he bent forward and peered out through the windscreen and watched the tracks running ahead of the car and the looming strips of fog. What was she saying? She was saying that there were too many things that he didn't say, too many secrets. That he left her alone. What had he brought her here for? What had he married her for, if he was to leave her alone? She was breaking the glass. If he did not break the glass, then she must break it. Damn it, Claire. His shout filled the car. Beneath the glass there was more glass, always more glass, like the ice that he knew could be there beneath the snow. He howled then to silence her, but not looking at her but looking ahead trying to see the road, his hands hard on the wheel. And there was ice, on a bend that he took too fast, though he was going so slowly, though he was staring ahead so carefully, trying so hard to concentrate on the road. His hands were tight with the effort, stiff on the wheel, and the car skidded, almost in slow-motion, so slowly it was travel-ling, and his howl died and they came to rest in a snow-filled ditch.

It was as if the car itself was winded, all the air gone from it. For a moment, nothing to breathe.

Are you all right?

Yes. Her gloved hand reached to his that seemed stuck to the wheel. The headlamps lit a tall hedge, lumps of snow dislodging from the branches onto the bonnet of the car.

We're both all right then.

Yes.

We'll have to walk. Not far to walk though, we were nearly home. I can come back with the tractor and pull the car out in the morning. See the damage. I think it's just enough off the road, if anyone else comes.

They got out like suddenly sobered drunks and took the shopping from the car boot. At least they had a torch. They had had the sense to keep a torch in the car. On the verge they were knee-high in snow but they were soon back to the ruts where it was cleared. It wasn't quite dark. It would never be quite dark because of the snow, which also made their path visible, the slippery tracks showing black down a road which luckily they knew well.

They barely spoke for the rest of the evening. Claire went to bed before he did and turned out the light. He had it in his head now, what he might have said. But it was too late. If she was awake when he came upstairs she showed no sign. That was better, he thought. Best that he didn't tell her, any of it. She only knew about the heroes. She couldn't be expected to understand.

What the jungle saw

How narrow a dividing line there could be between amazement and tedium. You thought it extraordinary to be there,
with a piece of your mind. You saw it with wonder, like the
pictures you had looked at when you were a child. And then
it became your dull reality. Perhaps it was just the exhaustion.
The trek, the humidity, the constant tension of looking about,
the fear in any unusual or unidentifiable sound. Walking always
at the same pace as the others. The need to walk together, act
together, see together. Four men on patrol, meant to see as one.

Only Luke kept his amazement, constantly looking up, holding his gun limp, wide-eyed. Walter hissed to get his attention.
Japs're hardly likely to be up there, are they, boy?

Luke wanted to see a hornbill. Someone had told him there
were hornbills in the Naga Hills.

What do they look like?

Big black-and-white bird. Beak like – well, like a horn.
You'd know one if you saw one.

Right then. Eyes peeled. We'll keep a lookout for them too,
won't we? Tommy said. Luke didn't look up for a long time
after that.

The day before, they had encountered some villagers who

were hiding out in the jungle. They had their livestock with them, a small herd of mithun and half a dozen black pigs. The villagers had indicated that a party of Japs had passed close by, moving east, but they had seen no sign of them since. Neither hide nor hair. That was a hunter's phrase, wasn't it, neither hide nor hair? He hadn't thought of that before. It was just one of those pointless idioms people liked to use. Rider Haggard probably used it. There was time between one pace and the next to let thoughts run, forward and back, so removed he was from all of the rest of his life.

When they heard the Jap he didn't sound like a man. The sound he made was more like one of those pigs, a sort of snorting and grunting, as he came towards them through the undergrowth, half hunched, hands in the air.

Ugly. Hair and hide. Perhaps it was his fear that made him ugly. Blubbing, grunting, shaking, a little scrawny bow-legged fellow with round specs clouded over. Falling on the ground in front of them. The sight of him made all of that battle crash back into his head, the battle that he had left behind, that they had all four of them left behind when they had entered this green. The hell-hole, the mud, the slaughter, all flooded in again about this wretched grovelling man. Those sounds must be words, grunting Japanese words like words they had heard in the battle. Only he didn't speak to them, but to the ground, to the trees to his side, behind their shoulders, to the ground again, his face distorted as he removed his specs and wiped his eyes. Probably he could

barely see anyway without the specs, the glass on them was
so thick.

———

We have to take him prisoner, one says, holding all that back.
One says it because one knows it's what one's supposed to say.
A man with his hands in the air is surrendering, even if Japs
don't surrender.

———

Maybe it was just a ruse and there were other Japs right by
them, waiting, watching, but this man seemed so abject that
you just had to believe in him.

Taking him prisoner was the only thing to do. Or was it?
What were the rules for such a situation, out here? Tommy
and Luke were closest. They moved forward, pulled him
up from where he grovelled, tied his hands behind his
back, but slowly, without conviction. What was the point
of taking a prisoner here, of tying a man's hands, when you
were nowhere and had nowhere to go? You took him prisoner simply because you could not leave him where he was
and alive. That would have been careless, stupid. But stupid
also to take him with you. You led him on along the track,
stumbling behind, and when you stopped you shared your

water with him, and he wiped his mouth with the muddied backs of his tied hands so that his face became muddy too, and after a while one of you untied his hands because he was stumbling so much and holding you all back, and he grunted some thanks. And he muttered and grunted in that language of his, for all your efforts to hush him, you knowing all the time the need to be silent, knowing that in the jungle sound made a man visible and that only silence allowed him to see.

Then you had him quiet for a stretch. Five of you then, not four, but walking as before, he making no more or less noise than anyone else. Five men in step, and the dullness returning.

Until something alarmed him. Did he hear something, some call that you took to be a bird call but was actually some sign they had? Or possibly he recognised some point on the track. Most likely it was that, that he noticed some tree or rock and suddenly knew where it was that they were going. Because he cracked again. Burst out into his gibberish.

Tommy, quick as a flash, put a hand across his mouth.

You all must have been thinking it, all four of you. But it was Tommy who took the initiative. Tommy who was so quick. Who would be most himself high above the saddle, bent to the horse's neck, whipping it on, no thought but for the finish.

Little Tommy was pretty much the same height as the other man. Stronger, though. The Jap was weak. He was not a young man anyway and he had the pinched look of a clerk, someone who had been desk-bound until he was brought out to this war, and the more feeble and pinched for all the time he had spent in the jungle. There was no contest.

You saw it, and in your mind, in the future, you would see it again and again.

Jap and jockey, two wiry little men clasped together, and one takes out his knife. And one folds over as the other steps back and raises his arm, fastidiously from what must no more be touched, and lets him go.

So quickly, it happened, and the rest of you saw it. You saw it and you heard it, heard a sound you'd never forget. The action happened in the space of a glance, you hearing, turning, seeing, the man folding and falling, all done before you could speak.

Only you didn't speak. You were silent.

Even the jungle seemed to have been silent, but for only that moment. Now the sounds started up again, loud, so loud, the insects and the birds and the monkeys, separate eerie calls from above and around and below them.

And Tommy said – with that cocky Newmarket look of his, or maybe defensive as much as cocky at that moment, chin up, eyes direct, face taut – Well we couldn't take him on any more, could we?

What could one say to that?

So they said nothing, but left it to the jungle. The jungle seemed to be saying what hadn't been said. The sounds must have been the same sounds that they had been hearing all day, only now the meaning of them was different. Strange, how the jungle's sounds could mean whatever you thought them to mean, as if all that wild and savage place became only the reflection of your thoughts. Before, it had been the jungle that was frightening. The jungle held the evil and the danger, it so vast about them and they so small within it, lost, searching. Sometimes there was a moment when the light and the sound magnified and there was hope. Here, the birds and the insects and the creatures had said. Here, this must be your way through, as the sun's rays penetrated from some sky high above. This is the way back to the rest of the force and safety. And then, as the air darkened once more, No, this isn't the way, this isn't your place, this is not your world, not for your kind. This is nature and you are nothing. You, your footsteps, your guns, are utterly insignificant.

Small, they were. Even smaller, whatever paltry argument of necessity they might offer in their defence. When wrong was done, the jungle knew.

Walter was walking again, and the rest of them had fallen in behind him. It was the four of them again now, and the jungle went on speaking.

That was when Walter lost the path and led them into the thorny bamboos. He couldn't have been watching where he was going. None of them perhaps was watching too well just then. When they got out from the thicket and the vegetation opened up they searched and found the path again, more focused now. They fell back into diamond formation, Walter ahead, he to one side, Luke at the rear, Tommy away to the other side where they did not have to face him. There was that thicket between them now and what they had left behind. But still, none of them could quite face him.

———

He wouldn't have had a word for it then. He had one now. He had it from Hussey and Hussey had it from the Nagas. It was *genna*, wasn't it? There were rules one played by, and it didn't do to break the rules.

Though actually, what happened next didn't need any special explanation. If you looked at it rationally, it could all be connected, the one event to the other, cause and effect, plus just an element of chance.

This thing with the Sikhs might have been why the Jap had fled, come to them blubbing, and why he had cracked again when he saw that they had come close to the spot.

Tommy saw first and whistled.

A single sharp bird-like note, but there seemed to be a kind of self-justification in it. See, this is what Japs do.

That miserable little man must have had something to do with this.

There would have been some sense in that.

Yet when he looked inside himself it seemed to him that all that was to follow was a consequence of what had just been done, or not consequence but intertwining. All these events intertwined.

———

They took every caution with their approach. They circled without a sound. First the Jap, and now this. They had known that he could not have existed entirely alone. That was why Tommy had done what he had done. Where one Jap was, there must have been others, other Japs about not so far away or long before. There had been the tracks they had followed. Now there was this clearing. They circled until they were sure that the space was empty – empty, that is, save for the death it contained, a bare clearing in the jungle that had been a Jap camp, and all that was left were marks on the ground and the remains of a fire and the Sikhs, and nothing alive. They had been tied with their turbans, their bared heads falling forward, the beards and the long loosed black hair, their torsos tied round and round with the khaki cloth, the cloth knotted and the loose ends falling away ribboning into the mud.

There was barbed wire twisted about their heads. You'd think the Japs would have used the turbans as blindfolds and the wire to tie, but no, they hadn't done that. Two of them had their eyes gouged out by the wire. The third had seen, and his eyes were open still.

The horror went to their guts. Over the hum of the flies came the crude human sound of Luke vomiting.

Words dropped heavy as stones.

Devils.

They must be close.

How close?

Can't leave these men here. Take out your spades and dig.

What about the Japs?

They've gone, haven't they?

But these chaps, they must be Hindus? Don't they get cremated or something?

Hindus, whatever they are, they're men.

Walter spoke as he would have wanted to speak before. Walter's face stern, the hollows on his cheeks running deep, Walter in that minute seeming stern as a preacher in a pulpit.

They're men and we'll bury them as we'd like to be buried ourselves.

———

As if decency could mend atrocity.

Oh Walter.

Did Walter see the pattern too?

———

Three graves to be dug and they had been digging in turn, digging hard and fast, each of them in turn standing lookout. They weren't digging the graves deep but even so there were numerous roots to be broken through close to the surface, and it had taken an undue amount of time. He had handed his spade to Tommy and walked a distance up to the edge of what had been the Jap camp, and taken out a new bundle of bidis to have a smoke, and as he walked the mist came in between him and the others. Mist could move here in the high jungle suddenly and unpredictably, as if it had a will of its own. He heard someone swear. Luke, maybe. Luke was the closest to where he stood, the others working on the graves just below. Luke had got bolder since they'd been on patrol. He was going to make a good soldier after all. Now we're in the bloody clouds, whoever it was – most probably Luke – said. The digging becoming the more determined. Surely they were deep enough now? They were all of them impatient to move on and make camp somewhere else. They did not want to spend the night here with the ghosts.

He tore the paper from the bidis, put one to his mouth. These little Indian matches were poor enough anyway, having to be struck away from the body in case they broke, then nurtured in a cupped hand, making it a job to get the bidi alight in the damp of the enclosing cloud. From below came the sound of the spades. Only with hindsight would he hear the Japs coming. At the time it seemed almost that it was the mist itself that was making the sound, moving down on them so thickly between the trees.

But there was no mistaking the shrieks. He knew them exactly. He had heard them before, in battle. The cries that the Japs made in attack.

Take cover.

Crouch down, the wood of a tree between you and the sound. One hand to the tree, to the damp bark, the red tip of the bidi put out amid the leaves at your feet.

See the sounds: shadows turning into leaping splay-kneed grotesques with shrieking mouths and bulging eyes, thrusting with bayonets and thrashing with swords.

Hear a cry that is recognisably Luke's. See Luke coming out of the cloud, close to your tree, Luke the graceful runner, running towards you, half his face cut off yet still he is running, so close to you he runs before he falls.

You have your gun in your hand by now, but there is only mist into which to shoot, white, thick, blinding. And if you shoot then they'll know that you're there. Because they might not know you exist. They might think there are only three soldiers, not four. They might never have seen you coming.

So he didn't shoot after all. He did nothing but run, run upwards first through the trees, telling himself that he would circle back, he would find a break in the mist and the trees through which he would turn and come back and fight. And he kept running and stumbling upwards and upwards, and the trees seemed to close behind and to the side of him and not to let him through, and the mist never broke, and he ran and ran.

When he stopped, the shrieking was over. He didn't know if he stopped because it ended or if it had ended while he was running. He listened now to the quiet that seemed to close in around him. He heard sporadic harsh calls from the Japs that seemed to get closer together and then recede. He tried to place them, the way they went. Then after a while he didn't hear them. Once the quiet was complete there was no distance any more. He dared not move. He didn't know how far he had run. He had come in the only direction that had seemed open to him, stopped at last at a point where creepers twisted together in a wall across his path, and there he stayed, until suddenly the mist turned to darkness. It happened in an instant. After that he couldn't very well go anywhere, but only hunker down in a night that was like dank black velvet and wait out the hours, and try to empty his mind and make that dark too.

The blankness lasted a breath at a time. He inhaled. Exhaled. Felt all of his body trembling. Felt the sweat chill on him, on his skin and in his clothes. Then the horror came back.

He turned to reason. Reason wasn't sleep but it was calm. Order. Man-made and measurable, like the minutes. He reasoned so deliberately that almost he saw the shapes of the words he was telling himself as he told them. His being there was sheer bloody fluke. It was one of those damn chances that saved a life, that he had exchanged places with Tommy just then – damn chance again, bloody, stupid fluke that he had wanted a smoke just then, and that they had finished a short time earlier the last of the bidis he carried on him, so that he had picked up his pack to get out another bundle of bidis, so that he had his pack and his water bottle and even some rations, and his blanket and his cape. All of his kit except his spade. His spade had been left behind. Poor bloody Tommy had his spade. Don't think, just don't think, not of Tommy, not of any of them. Don't think of the digging or of Walter or the graves or the Sikhs, or of Tommy and the Jap, before. That way thoughts are no longer words but pictures, and pictures you cannot deal with, not right now, maybe not ever.

He heard dawn before he saw it, a signal passed down from high in the canopy where for the birds at least there must be sky. Down on the underfloor there was only a seep of light. He looked about him in the blur, packed up his things, rolled up the blanket and cape with which he had wrapped himself and strapped them to his pack. Everything there, all neat, except for the spade. But that didn't matter, did it? A soldier needed his spade only to bury his shit, and his comrades. And he didn't feel like a soldier any more, not here, not now. He felt no more than a man, or an animal, only an animal crouched on the forest floor watching for the dawn. Which way had he come? He knew that he had climbed upwards, so he looked down the slope. He had run in panic. Everywhere he looked, it looked the same. He could find no track of himself on the ground. There was a compass in his pocket but it could not give him the directions that mattered, if he wanted to find the place where they had been. He had come up. If he wanted to go back, he must go down. If he wanted to go back, to find them. That simple thing was clear. So he would go down. But should he go straight, or to the right, or to the left? There was something else they had been taught in training, that when men were lost one man tended to veer to the right and another to the left. Which way then should he go, if he was to find them? What sort of man was he? And what was he looking for and what would he find and what would he do when he found it? They were surely dead. The spade then, he would have to find the spade. His spade – or someone else's spade would do. But there were graves already dug. He thought that they would not mind sharing graves, with only one man there to dig. Three graves. Three Sikhs. Three British soldiers. The spade then would be only for filling the graves. But why all this burying, what need was there? Because Walter must do it. If Walter saw the need, then he must do what Walter wanted. Walter would have them do it because of what had gone before, because of what the four of them had done – and it was four, wasn't it, not Tommy alone?

What Tommy had done, the four of them had done. All for one and one for all. That was how the words went, wasn't it? The words came from a story he once knew. Men with swords and curling feathers in their hats. Three Musketeers, and D'Artagnan, four men in all, and one survives.

Was it possible that any of the others had survived? He must see, and at least he must bury. And if he was the only one, then he would carry the memory for the four of them. All for one. It would be his, all his, to carry on.

He checked his watch, reckoned the time he had spent searching. He had tried to search systematically, as far as the vegetation permitted, zigzagging down the slope, trying to control his direction and his thoughts, this way and that but always down, always looking about him, covering what must surely be a wide enough swathe of ground.

Incrementally, it seemed, the mist had thinned as he walked, one layer removed and then another, and as it thinned he heard increasingly the chitter of insects, and birds close above him, enlivened by the light. But it was a tenuous grey light that would soon turn to rain. The living sounds died, to be replaced by the sound of rain on the canopy, rain that hammered the tops of the trees and then washed down between the leaves, erratic at first, held where the leaves were most dense, finding its way along and between and pouring through the openings, then converging in streams on the forest floor, destroying whatever tracks remained, if he could have found them, pouring over whatever lay there on the ground, stumps, rotten branches like bodies, as if there was only one element to which everything must return. And he had his rain cape, and though the water streamed down his face, his body within the cape was dry. He had never felt so entirely alone as he did beneath that rain, with his cape over his head and the world dissolving about him. After three hours he abandoned the search. He took a compass bearing and determined what he thought was most likely to be the direction of the British force.

Most courageous are the Belgae

An airmail envelope. A sheet of onionskin paper scrawled in Hussey's tight slanting script.

Mokokchung, 14 December 1947

My dear Charlie,

I hope demob life is treating you well. I shall be back myself sometime in March, the first time I'll have been back in poor old England since before the war. I will be handing over shortly to my Indian replacement. Goodness only knows what he'll make of it, he'll be as alien to the place as I ever was, coming up from the plains – and there's no kind of man a Naga distrusts more than the Indian from the plains. I think they don't give a damn about us, in either London or Delhi – or I don't mean myself, but the Nagas, who are nothing but a nuisance to them all. So much easier it would be if they just disappeared into the jungle and the past. But enough of that. I can bore you with that when I see you. What I wondered was whether I might take you up, when I do get home, on your possibly careless invitation of some time ago, and come and see you and see your farm? What a good thing that must be to be doing, these days of all days, to be working the land. The best, in fact. My regards to your wife. It will be a pleasure to meet her.

Yours

Jack

Chap I stayed with in Nagaland. ICS. They're sending him home.

I suppose they'll all have to come home now, she said.

It'll hardly be home to him, will it? He must have lived in India longer than he ever lived in England. They have a way out there of talking about England as home even if they'd hardly recognise the place.

He had thought it in the summer, hearing the news from India. We are leaving India, he had thought. So Hussey must come home now. When the second thought came to him it had seemed a second loss.

He wants to come and see us.

Then we must have him to stay. When's he coming?

He doesn't say.

Tell him he can come any time. She put a hand to her belly. She was six months pregnant, the bump already big on her slight frame. Let's hope it's before the baby's due.

Yes, he said, though the thought came to him that he might use the baby as some excuse, so that he might not come.

Does he have a wife? You've hardly told me anything about him.

There was a wife once. She died. There's a grown-up son somewhere.

He knew the wife's name. Eleanor Mary Hussey. He had seen her grave outside the little white church at Mokokchung. There was the son, schooled in England and enlisted shortly before the end of the war, and a Sema Naga girl – not girl, woman, rather round and merry, not by any means a beauty – often at the bungalow when Hussey was there, and she went back to her village when he went on tour. So little he had learned of Hussey's personal life, in all the weeks that he had lived with him. Strange to think that Hussey and Eleanor, Eleanor Mary, had been through what he and Claire were going through, knowing this potential, the beginning of family. You did not see anything of it in him.

He signs himself Jack, he said, I've never thought of him as that. Only Hussey.

Good Lord! the man had said. Taking his feet from the chair, taking the pipe from his mouth. A tall oddly familiar kind of Englishman, bony, a little unkempt, the look on him, even at first sight, of a man who lived alone. And where have you come from?

Hussey, coming here. He had issued the invitation in good faith, he had such a gratitude to the man, yet he had not expected him to come. He had thought Hussey somehow immune; as if he would stay up there for ever, in his high bungalow, smoking his pipe, studying his Nagas, typing out his ethnographic studies in the small hours of the night. Those nights when he had lived there, when he was so much awake and sleep was so erratic, he had found comfort in the sound that came through the thin walls, of Hussey typing away, typing amateurishly with two fingers on his big black typewriter, typing out observations that sometimes he would give him to read the next day, on flimsy white paper with a smudged and much corrected carbon copy, that one for himself and the top one for London. He had imagined permanence, certainty of purpose, in the little flurries of clacking, the return, the pauses, the seep of tobacco smoke through the darkened house.

There had been terrible reports from India this last year. Riots. Killings, in cities and villages, horrifying in their nature and in their unthinkable number. People pulled from trains, in unthinkable numbers, and killed by the tracks. He had read those things, here in England where they were so far away, and even here he could picture them. (So many things he could picture nowadays. Words came to him as pictures and he couldn't blank the pictures out and return them to words.) He knew how it looked, how it would look. He knew how the cities must have looked, the streets and the open drains where the words had said that all those bodies lay – and the trains, he knew the open glassless windows of the trains, the long hot embankments, the vast land that stretched out away from the tracks, the figures on the land – and the words told him of the people on the trains, the grappling hands at the windows, the people killed where they sat, or dragged out; how they lay slaughtered, in white cloth and bright sari cloth, along the side of the line. The vultures. The flies.

He had known that. The words told him that, small print in black and white. But the words told him that the killings, like the politics, were things mainly of the Indians and the plains. He had pictured all that, and he had pictured Hussey up in his sea of blue hills, utterly removed from it all. Clouds between them.

The letter was followed by a postcard from Cairo a couple of months later. Hussey had reached the Pyramids. Good for him, he thought, he must be spinning out the journey home. There would be no urgency to his returning to the place that he called home but wasn't really. Might as well see a pyramid or two – or three, there were three pyramids at Giza, weren't there? Three in the postcard, certainly, and a palm tree and a camel. Hand-coloured sand and a streak of turquoise in the sky. Then, the same day that the postcard came, there was a telephone call. It seemed too soon, that the man had travelled as fast as the card.

That's quick.

What's quick?

That was Hussey. He wants to come this Thursday. I'm sorry, I didn't think he'd be here so soon. Perhaps he hadn't really expected that he would ever arrive.

What do you think he'd like to eat, your friend, if he's been in India all this time?

The food there had been the plainest, cooked by the merry woman, plain boiled things but the hottest chillies to go with them.

Whisky soda, that's what he likes.

Roll upon roll of hills, the lone white man on his veranda overseeing all. Stretched out in the planter's chair, whisky glass, pipe to his mouth. Rainstorm passed, leaves shining, the powerful smell of suddenly wet earth. Clouds breaking up and whisking themselves away as they did only in places so high. Watching the clouds clearing from the hills, the man will be able to see from a long way off the little cavalcade making its way towards him, winding down the slope opposite, then out of sight in the dip of the valley, identifiable, as it climbs up to where he is, as another lone white man and two Nagas, but its macabre nature not known until they reach the lawn and the roses and the marigolds. Well might he say, Good Lord! The stink of the head will have got to him even amid the pipe smoke.

Easy to spot him on the railway platform by his stillness. Everyone else was on the move. He had his back to the gate, a stiff figure in a rather roomy new overcoat and a dark trilby, but Charlie knew him at once.

Hussey, over here!

A clasping of hands. Good to see you, old boy.

I'm sorry, I didn't want to keep you waiting.

The train only just got in.

Let me take this.

The suitcase spoke of where he had come from, the hard brown leather worn soft at the corners, scuffed and scratched, but the handle, as Charlie put his hand to it, little used. It was a suitcase that had been carried on men's heads and not in their hands.

How was the journey?

Fine.

He took the case to the car, placed it on the ground, opened the boot, lifted it in, Hussey standing the while by the passenger door. Charlie got in his side and leant across to open it for him.

Well, let's go.

It was difficult to know where to begin. The car's engine seemed loud, each change of gear noticeable. Hussey looked out at the landscape.

Is it far?

Not far.

Tell me when we get to your land.

As they approached the house Claire came out to meet them.

From the way Charlie had spoken of him, she had been expecting someone more substantial. This man was thin and sallow. His hand shaking hers was dry as paper. His eyes on her made her more than ever aware of her fullness. I didn't know, he said, Charlie didn't tell me. Congratulations.

Oh, not long to go now, she said. She thought it might embarrass him to say how very soon she was due. I'm sorry, I look like a whale. But actually she felt rather grand and stately before him.

He had brought them a gift. A beautiful thing, he thought. He hoped they would see the beauty in it. Sometimes it seemed to him that what was beautiful there was lost on people here.

He gave it to them when he came down for a drink before supper. They had all bathed and changed. The fire was burning high in the grate. Claire had on a dark red dress that clashed just so slightly with her lipstick, and Charlie looked sleek and clean, a little pink. He had filled out in the last three years, a solidity to him that must be partly health and coming home but was also his physical way of life. He was beginning to look like the Norfolk farmer he had become. He knew that he must feel glad for him, because this should be an enviable existence.

Whisky soda?

Yes, please.

Ice?

No, no ice.

The drink amber in a cut-glass tumbler. Glint of light on it.

He had looked at the land from the train. There had not been a hill all the way from London. Then from the car, as Charlie drove. Dull, tamed land, he had thought, almost every square yard of it productive. No jungle here, none of that age-old battle to hold the jungle back. They turned off the main road.

Tell me when we get to your land, he had said, wanting to know where Charlie's farm began, and Charlie told him when they got to the hedge that formed the boundary. This is our land now, on this left side of the road, all ours from now on, and he saw how one field, whoever it belonged to, very much resembled another. But then there was the house, set at the heart of its land, and this pretty, hugely pregnant woman standing in the porch. So much purpose. And he thought that owning land in itself was purpose. Just putting your feet on it would hold you down. Because he himself was floating. He had been floating in London, through all the people on the grey streets, even in the club, where there were others India-returned as he was and floating too, as they read *The Times* in their leather armchairs and recognised the symptoms of it in each other, and repeated familiar phrases in the attempt to fix themselves, the phrases already becoming a little absurd or contrived. What was a chota peg once you were home but a little glass of whisky?

I've brought you this, from Nagaland. He pulled it out from his pocket and offered it to Claire, and she took it tentatively. It was the head of a mithun carved in some blackish wood, small enough to fit in the palm of her hand, a piece of orange string running through a loop at the back of it that must once have held it around a man's neck.

A bull's head?

Not a bull exactly, a mithun. Mithun are the cattle they have there. But much like a bull.

She turned it about, strange in her Englishwoman's hands, a smooth stylised bull's head with long horns, burnished and greasy from the skin of the man who had worn it, who touched it before she touched it, and blackened further by the smoke of the huts. Everything that ever went indoors in Nagaland had a little of that sooty coating, and a smell that clung to it even when you took it out and transported it elsewhere.

Why, it's like a little piece of modern art, she said. A Henry Moore or something. Thank you so much. And she put it up on the mantelpiece between the figurines.

He was disappointed to see it there. Of course, it will dry out here, he thought, and the smell will fade. The life will be gone from it.

He assumed that the figurines beside which it seemed so incongruous were hers, to her taste, that she was the sort of woman who lived in this sort of house. And that her answer was no more than politeness.

They ate in the dining room.

I hope it's not too chilly for you, his hostess said, thinking as people in England always thought that he had come from a climate of constant heat. No, no, it's fine, I'm quite acclimatised, he replied, though the room was in fact a little chilly. It was Claire who he thought must feel the cold most, in her dress. He supposed the pregnancy kept her warm. Or just the colour of the dress. She looked warm, with her dark curled hair and brown eyes, at the end of the table closest to the sideboard, pulling herself heavily up to bring a ladle for the gravy. Charlie stood at the sideboard and carved a joint of beef. He felt that he should do something, left sitting alone at the mahogany table with the candles and silver things upon it. It was so long since he had been in such a place.

He did look cold. There was a draught even when the door was closed. Better if they had eaten in the kitchen. She had thought it necessary somehow to have supper here but it made the evening too formal. This room wasn't friendly. It would be the first room she would redecorate, when they had the money. She would have it red, wine-coloured. Red dining rooms were more intimate. She thought this as the two men talked, the conversation passing about her, she eating slowly, but greedily because of the baby, aligning the knife and fork straight on her plate when she had finished, folding the white linen napkin and placing it tidily on the polished wood, resting her hand there, waiting until they were finished too, wondering when they would be ready for pudding or cheese. Were they saying what they wanted to say? The talk was men's talk, club talk, without personal meaning. They talked about India's Independence. There had been so much talk of that, this year just passed. But what Hussey said was different. He said that Independence hadn't pleased the Nagas. For a moment she was caught by the conversation. When Gandhi was killed, he said, when he was already in Kohima on his way home, he had heard a Naga laugh aloud.

But why? she asked, seeking explanation. Perhaps her voice was too light, because they didn't hear her, and didn't answer, as if her words were only for herself.

Other things caught. The notion of the Union Jack coming down, fluttering as it folded. That the population of tigers had increased since the war – either that, or the tigers had increased their attacks on humans, having become habituated to human flesh, so much of it there was, strewn around. How horrid, that. She passed the cheeseboard. She had managed to be generous with the dinner, despite rationing. Yes, this was Stilton. Ah, Hussey said, he hadn't tasted real Stilton for years.

As she put out the cheese Charlie remembered that there was some port. He went out to the kitchen, found the bottle and two small glasses. Came back into a silence.

There was something I remember I said once. About the Nagas. I think it was rather romantic.

She was outside the conversation now. Not drinking. Withdrawn into the company of the baby, one hand resting unselfconsciously on her bump.

I think I said they were noble. They aren't really, are they? They're just like anyone else.

Oh, said Hussey. In some ways I think they are.

So he was in love with them too.

It *is* cold in here, she said. Let's go through to the sitting room.

She led them through, moving sedately, going forward to take the guard from the fire.

Let me. You shouldn't be doing that, darling.

The two men sat in armchairs on either side of the fire-place, Claire on the sofa facing it. She kicked off her shoes and curled up with a cushion against her.

They sound rather horrid to me, your Nagas, not noble at all. But she spoke rather sweetly and smiled, so that it was clear that she didn't mean him to take offence. The challenge was not to him but to Charlie, in that secret place that he kept from her.

Ah, well, they do have a terrifying reputation.

She would draw this man out, since he was here, whom Charlie spoke of as so wise.

You have to get to know them for yourself, isn't that so, Charlie?

She would tell him to fill his glass again and talk, Charlie silent in the other chair thinking whatever he thought, looking into the fire.

Things were changing, he said with a touch of regret. Many of the Nagas were hymn-singing Baptists now. There had been American missionaries all over the place, building chapels, teaching them hymns, making them wear clothes as if their nakedness had been a sin. Though he had still had to deal with head-takings now and then.

How did he 'deal with' head-takers, she wondered, this pale bookish man out there in the jungle? So scarcely credible it seemed, this world that he spoke of. Anyway, wasn't head-taking just murder?

No, not there, he said. There it was not murder but accepted, like disease, or a traffic accident, or war. Though of course it seemed like murder. Of course one might well see it as murder, particularly when it was a case of some woman a raiding party had caught out in the fields, or a child who had been taken captive.

Oh God, but that's utterly barbaric.

Hussey put down his glass and leant forward, elbows to his knees and long pale hands paired before him. Like one of those missionaries. How unexpected it was, this conversation earnestly followed in this room which was still not really her room, but Ralph's room, like a waiting room or rather a room in a house in which they were all of them guests coming from their different places and passing through. Or through which Hussey was passing, while they two were long-term residents, becalmed before the ticking clock, the reflections in the mirror, shocking her with his macabre and not entirely believable traveller's tale. Don't get me wrong, though, the traveller was saying, in his thin dry voice. In the old days, in the average Naga village, a loss of more than one or two heads a year would have been considered singularly unlucky. It was as if they lived in a constant state of war, but only a simmering kind of war, and one that was bound about with rules and rituals. What they called *genna*. Think about it. War's a way of being, isn't it? It's like a religion. It brings people together, gives shape and purpose to everything. And life's not the same when it's gone. There was an essay he had read, he could send it to her if she liked, by an ethnographer in Melanesia, who observed how when head-hunters were deprived of headhunting they lost their zest for life. That was the phrase the ethnographer used, that was the phrase precisely. He had never met people anywhere with such zest for life as the Nagas.

Heads were everything, he said. Heads were power. Heads were the source of a tribe's meaning and its art. The possession of heads meant fertility, for men and for their crops. It was prophylactic against disease. All skulls contained the magic they needed. All were equally efficacious, and in times of need a newly taken skull might be broken up and the fragments shared or traded between clans or even allied tribes, the front parts most valued as these held the most power.

Oh God, she thought, feeling the baby within her, its skull so complete, pressing deep in her womb. She looked to Charlie but he wasn't seeing her. He was caught up in some thought of his own.

The doctor had said that the baby had turned – he or she – his head, her head, in position, ready, almost, to come out into the world. It was so big now that its movements were no longer somersaults or kicks but upheavals in the depths of her, where she had not known she could feel. She must go now, she thought. He or she – they, herself as well – they two, she and the baby, must remove themselves from this room where the words disturbed her in her depths, take themselves to bed, to silence and darkness and sleep.

Why, look at the clock, it's late, I really must go up now. Yawning, lifting herself, saying goodnight. I put water in your room. I think that you should have everything you need.

It's not true, what you say. Charlie had watched her padding away, the fragile weight of her that he found at that moment so beautiful. He did not speak until the door was closed. *It's all murder. War, whatever. Whatever you choose to call it.*

Hussey leant further forward and bowed his head in his hands. He began speaking like that, through his hands, and then raised his head and there was pain in his eyes.

A terrible thing happened just before I left. I suppose, in a way, we knew it was coming. It had been building, I suppose, for months. All through the war it had been becoming more possible. Everything was disturbed. People had fled to the jungle. Crops hadn't been planted, or where they had, the Japs came through and took everything, slaughtered the mithun, the chickens, any of the people who resisted. How could we expect that once the war was over there would be nothing but peace?

And there were the guns. We'd flooded the place with guns. For every dead soldier in the jungle, a gun. A trail of dead soldiers and of guns all the way into Burma. It wasn't only the tigers that benefited from all the dead. You know how I used to try to control the spread of guns? Well, we weren't going to be around to do that any more, were we? We weren't going to be there to keep order, to carry out our punitive raids, to do anything at all. Everyone knew that. There was talk. All last year there was talk. We were up in the mountains, as if we were in another country. We'd been a long way from the horrors in Calcutta, we were further still from the Punjab, but the news got to us all the same. The British were leaving, and everyone was killing everyone.

There was an old chief who came to me. His name was Chui-ong. The Raj is gone, he said. Sir, we must all have guns. Or we will be gone too. Finished like you. But we last remnant of the Raj stuck to our principles – I nearly said guns, Charlie, that we stuck to our guns. Of course, we are British and we stick to our guns. Even at a time like that, when actually we are sneaking away, we have to keep up appearances, don't we? So we stuck to our guns and no, we didn't give them guns. In fact, we took their guns away. Because that was our policy. Don't let children play with dangerous toys. Don't worry if other children have them next door. We're better than them. It's the principle that counts.

I stayed on, as you know, last autumn. We were gone, but we weren't gone. I was still in post. Not Britain behind me but the new India now, men in Delhi who had never heard of Nagas and didn't feel any debt to them for their help in the war.

Another chief came to me. You should have seen him. A regal figure in a blanket covered with large printed tigers, clamouring for guns. Did he want them to defend his village or to raid another, or to start a war for independence from India? I didn't know. I wasn't giving out any guns. I had my orders. I even went to his village later and took what guns he had away. Why do you do this, sir? he said. I think I tried to say something about peace. Your British peace is not our peace, he said. Of course I knew that he was right. It never was, was it?

I don't know, Charlie said. I thought that was what you were doing, *Pax Britannica* and all that.

I thought we'd achieved something there. That our presence, the flag, meant something. But it didn't, did it? There were cracks all along, only we chose not to see them. And a society can break apart so fast.

There was a pause in which Charlie heard no more than the wuther of the flames. Claire had left her shoes askew on the red rug at the foot of the sofa.

We had been drawing our nice little lines. Peace here, just so far, then a line. Beyond, the barbarians.

Like Hadrian.

Only we didn't build a wall. We didn't protect them on our side.

No.

How do you draw a line across civilisation, anyway? Set some boundary, wherever it seems practical, civilise the people on one side of it and not those on the other? It was all so arbitrary.

Charlie had not known there was such anger in him. He had thought Hussey a type of the colonial official, emanating security and calm.

I hadn't seen it like that.

No, of course you hadn't. No one did. It doesn't suit to see it that way. The truth was, civilising a village just made it vulnerable to attack. All the more so if it seemed peaceful and prosperous. The next village along just became more envious, envious of the others' lives, their crops, their heads.

Yes, now you say it, I see, of course, Charlie said. He thought of the village where he had stayed. How he would have envied that. But by Hussey's argument it didn't count.

It must have been beyond the wall, if there had been a wall. Lucky village. If only it would remain so.

Mind if I light a pipe?

Go ahead, Charlie said. Another drink?

No.

But Charlie had the bottle already in his hand.

Yes then, why not?

They sat in silence for a while. There was the fire, the slow tick of the clock between the mithun head and the figurines, the odd creaks of the old farmhouse. Claire's shoes on the floor. She had gone padding upstairs, Charlie thought, like a Naga. Now that she was pregnant she carried her weight differently, like those women there. Or perhaps it was only that she had given up wearing high heels, he thought, perhaps that was all the difference. A pregnant woman was a pregnant woman, anywhere. That quiet power in them, something invulnerable despite their vulnerability. Some ancient piece of goddess.

You didn't tell me what happened.

What? Hussey's eyes were on the floor as well. On that little sign of the woman present but gone.

The terrible thing.

No, I didn't, did I?

The story began on the veranda. Hussey called outside before he had finished his breakfast. The valley filled with morning mist, layers of cloud above, and away to the east a dark column of smoke, rising into the cloud and turning it brown and yellow and sullen.

You remember where Choknyu was?

Choknyu? I'm not sure that I do. Did we go there?

It's a village on a ridge to the east. Just outside our administrative district. We trekked there one day, went to see an old rascal of a chief sodden with opium.

Oh yes, I remember now.

It was on fire. The whole village was burning. A hundred houses and granaries all going up together. The flames so tall that you could see them from where we were, so far off, streaks of orange beneath the smoke. Strange though, you couldn't hear a thing. Somehow if you see something like that you expect to hear, but there was only the fire and the smoke and the cloud, and the meaning of it.

Hussey standing on the veranda. Everyone from the bungalow gathered there, watching. Below them in the town they haven't seen it yet. The morning goes on as mornings do in Mokokchung, the sounds the usual sounds of people and dogs and chickens, and maybe someone cutting wood.

What did you do?

There was nothing I could do. Not straight away. We just watched. We knew what was there, all those headless corpses that would be lying there. I might have put a party together, sent it off in hot pursuit. Perhaps they would have caught up with the raiders, I don't know. But I had to telegraph for permission to enter the area. So we watched, Charlie. We watched in utter and abject horror. Now and then a new building caught alight, and there were new flames and another column of smoke, and then the fire would die back and blend in again with the clouds. It was too late anyway. The damage was done.

Even as they first saw it, the climax of the raid was past. The heads were already taken. The burning would be the end of it. What could Hussey have done but make a show? Keep up for one last moment the façade of rule. As it was, he waited for his permission and then he did assemble men, and they marched the three hours, down into the valley and up to the village as it still burned. And all along the march they met others who had seen the smoke, who shouted to them in excitement. That was why the façade still mattered. Why it had to be kept up. Because the people were as excited about the raid as their ancestors would ever have been. Civilisation had only damped them down. There was nothing so much as a headhunting raid, Hussey said, to rekindle zest for life. He saw proof of it now. He accepted that was the theory, what the anthropologists said, but somehow he had not expected it of his own people, of people whose faces and names he knew, and even ones he'd seen going to church. Perhaps it is always so, that you expect that others, even when you know that they are different, will see the world as you do. Share your taboos and your horrors. But it was not so. For days to come, villages in the region would be celebrating the great raid, beating drums and dancing, some of them trading with the raiders for heads and parts of heads.

Hussey's voice was worn out. He needed the wet of the whisky just to speak any more. His look drifted across the floor. Charlie wasn't sure that he was seeing anything in the room any more, not himself, not the rug, not Claire's shoes. Claire and her kind were outside all that mattered to Hussey now; Claire, women, family, things of his past. What had mattered to him these last years had all been bound up in his work: his people, the care of his people who seemed to him to be threatened by every influence that came their way – the bureaucrats and missionaries who wanted to change them, the anthropologists who wanted to isolate them – and his private work too, the study of his people, the notes he wrote up through those lonely nights, in those early mornings, clacking away at his typewriter, recording every detail he could find of a story over which he had no power. Hussey wasn't seeing what was before him here, the room, the house, the farm. He was only seeing the story. If he had briefly forgotten it at dinner, then he had remembered again now that it was late and the glow of the drink had faded and left him so low. How old was he? Fifty, sixty, Charlie wasn't sure. He looked very old now.

These people were like the crowd at the Colosseum, Hussey said. Only the spectacle was spontaneous and they hadn't had to buy tickets. We're a bloodthirsty lot, we humans.

Yes, Charlie answered. I think we are.

Silence then.

Was this why Hussey had taken up his invitation? To come here and tell him this? To tell his horror to another who had been where he had been and might understand, even if he wasn't there any more and was making himself into someone else, into some bluff Norfolk farmer who didn't think about those sorts of things any more. Who had come home intact, hair, fingernails and all, head on his neck, though his memory slipped now and then, jolted out into the open.

It was well past midnight. Charlie topped up the glasses once more, and then the fire, squatted a moment before it as a fresh log began to catch. Should these things be said, or not be said? If they were said in this dead time of the night, would the night take them away? As if the blackness might absorb the black and then in the morning it would be gone, but he also perhaps gone, sucked away in it.

Hussey spoke to his back. We were responsible, you know. I knew that, all the time we were marching there. It was our fault. My fault. There'd been some minor incident a couple of months earlier, the sort of petty head-taking that was going on all the time, that's been common these last few years, and to punish the village I had to go and take all their guns away. They couldn't even defend themselves. It was a massacre, you know. When we finally got there we counted four hundred bodies.

He didn't turn round. He didn't want to meet Hussey's eyes. No, he thought, the things shouldn't be said. How could you live in the morning with what you had said in the night?

Well, we've left now. You've left. What'll you do now?

I don't know. Retire, perhaps. There's only me, I could eke out my pension. There was a possibility of a post in Kenya but I don't know if I could start anywhere else.

The conversation was coming back to some kind of normality.

Have you been to Africa?

No. It would be quite new.

They say the Kenyan highlands are beautiful.

So are the Cotswolds.

Yes.

So much listening he had done. Not speaking but only seeing. Seeing what he did not want to see, things that seemed scarcely possible, seen from here. Drinking his drink. The fire dying down, his wife going to bed, this man here speaking whom he really did not know very well, who did not know him, did not know who he was here but only who he might have been somewhere else, whose dry words tugged at the nightmare, pulled it this way and that. Words were so dry, weren't they, always? No blood to them. No breath. Only bone. Empty skulls. And the bodies were left without heads. And the heads were taken away.

There was one last thing he suddenly thought to say, before they went to bed. He, like Hussey, was drunk, but so numbly now that he didn't know he was drunk any more.

You remember that fellow who came with me, he said, who brought the head? How did he take it, not getting his medal? I think I couldn't bear to ask you about him at the time.

Nonchalantly. Hussey said the word slowly, pausing on each syllable. The wretch just shrugged his shoulders and left. Didn't seem to think it was very serious. I was almost afraid he might come back later with another one. Like a cat dropping a mouse at your feet.

It was my fault.

Why?

If I hadn't turned up there, he wouldn't have had the idea.

Not your fault at all. His idea.

And then another thought struck him and he began to smile.

Do you know what I called him, to myself, what I called him from the moment I saw him? The scrum-half.

Did you know about the head when you called him that?

No.

Suddenly it was funny. He saw the burly little scrum-half running, dodging, passing between them, a small tank of a man. Zigzagging this way and that with the head like a rugger ball under his arm, diving to the ground, sliding on the green grass before the marigolds. Scoring a try.

Two men's laughter carried up the stairs.

Claire heard them through her sleep. How could they laugh? She woke from a dream. The baby was lying asleep on the jungle floor, and Charlie was abandoning it. She saw the back of him walking away laughing, a shadow ahead of him that might have been Hussey, and she stood by and could not pick it up, and though she did not see them, there were naked Nagas and tigers about them in the jungle. She woke, and felt for the baby's head. It must be there. She couldn't feel it yet she knew that it was there, wedged as the doctor said. What she could feel was not the baby's head but only its legs, doubled-up like those of a trussed chicken.

Her sleep was so broken these nights, disturbed by the baby or her bladder, or just the difficulty of making her body comfortable for any length of time. She felt that she had been aware for hours that they were still down there talking, hearing at moments the murmur of their voices from the sitting room, before this silly laughter and the creaking on the stairs. Now she had woken afraid. She didn't remember having any dreams these last months. She had thought this was because her body had taken over. She had come to know herself as an entirely physical creature, like an animal, with sharp sense of smell, sharp revulsions, sharp hungers, instinctive responses. But animals dreamt, didn't they? Dogs, anyway. It seemed to her that Jess had dreams, and sometimes stirred in them, and woke afraid. She turned again in the bed, moved to the side so that there would be space for Charlie, put a pillow beneath where she was most uncomfortable. She felt that the baby was awake now. Did the baby hear what she heard? There would be the hum of her own body first, between the baby and the silly men. She rested a hand where it was, low, where the pain most often came, close to the head.

When Charlie came into the bed he lay on his back and almost instantly began to snore. Gently she spoke to him and he obeyed, turned onto his side and was silent. She didn't sleep again for a long time. She lay awake keeping company with the baby.

Mrs T said it was a boy, because she was big behind, big all round. Mrs T talking away as she polished the dining-room table, bent over the gleaming mahogany as it would have been impossible for her to do now with all this bulk. You and Mr Ashe'll be wanting a boy, won't you, on account of the farm?

Someone to take over the farm, yes. But that was a long time off.

She had been used to envying the men since she had come to live here. Perhaps she had always envied the men the physicality of their existence. Men did and made. Men fought the war. Men farmed the land and came back in with their physical exhaustion and their physical satisfaction. She had felt insubstantial beside them, flimsy as the dresses she wore, the skirts that lifted and blew in the wind. That she must hold down with her hands.

Now with the baby there was gravity in her. The head low, the weight of the baby in the depths of her.

Yes, she had thought, a boy would be good. She would be grounded in boys.

It was at harvest time that she first knew that she was pregnant. The change in her came with a great tiredness that meant that she curled up and slept through stretches of the day when everyone was out in the fields and no one in the house to see. So she told no one at first. If Mrs T suspected, she did not speak of it. From the stillness of the house she could hear the harvesting, identify by the direction of the sound the field they had got to – she knew the farm well enough for that by now – hear the grain cart coming in and out of the yard, the voices of the men, and yet it seemed to have no connection to her, all that activity out there.

She told Charlie one evening when the harvest was almost done. It was late and the sun was low and they were walking the stubble. She had not known before she came here that stubble had different colours and textures, that barley stubble was more soft and golden than wheat. The harvest had been good. These last weeks had been dry, and the dry ground was cracked between the stalks. They walked the golden stubble and the cracks in the land.

I think I'm pregnant, she said, reaching for his hand.

Think, he said, or know?

I know, she said. I wasn't going to tell you until I was certain. You've been so busy. I think you've scarcely seen me these last few weeks.

Of course I've seen you. I always see you.

Charlie's hand was sure about hers, dry and hard and dusty.

But are you happy?

He stopped and took her other hand. They faced each other now.

Yes, I'm happy.

She wasn't sure, even when his arms were about her, the dusty grain-smell of him.

And now he slept hot and separate at her side.

After a time she felt the need again to get up. The baby pressed on her. She slipped away from Charlie's hot body and out of the room. She could make her way in the dark now, so many nights she had done this, out along the passage, quietly, without waking him or even waking herself any further by putting on any lights. But Hussey seemed to be awake. She could see a bright crack beneath the door of the spare bedroom.

Hussey heard the creak of the boards as she went to the bathroom, heard the flush, heard her go back. When he thought she must have settled, he got up himself, quietly, went to the bathroom and washed and shaved. He exchanged his pyjamas for the clothes he had taken off such a short time before, only with clean underwear, and a crisp clean shirt that had been ironed and folded at his club. There was barely anything to pack as so little had been unpacked the night before. He had been used to having a servant unpack for him, laying his things in drawers, removing them from drawers, bungalow to bungalow, when he was on tour. He took his case with him when he went downstairs.

In the kitchen the dog slept in a basket close to the stove. She uncurled and greeted him, her warmth and her smell about his legs. He bent to stroke her. Shhh, Jess, that's your name, isn't it? Then she curled again while he made tea, though the water was slow to boil.

He took a notebook from the top of his case and tore out a page, folding it first and taking a knife to the fold so that the edge was neat. Then he took out a fountain pen from the breast pocket of his jacket.

My dear Charlie,

The Cotswolds won't do. I see that, coming here. I must get to London and tell them this morning if I want the Kenya job. You have a good life here and I don't want to intrude on it. I wish you the best of luck. Please give my apologies to your lovely wife for being such a rude guest.

Jack

Two stiff black bolts on the back door, top and bottom. Hard to push them back without a sound. He turned the key in the lock, opened the door, trying to hold Jess back as he did so but she wriggled out beside the suitcase. No, you can't come with me, dog. But she did and he let her. She would turn back somewhere. Dogs always did. And this her place. She would know her way home.

It was foggy, the cobbles in the yard shiny with heavy cold dew. He walked out through the open gate, round to the drive and to the road. No, Jess, you can't come with me any more. He thought he should make a token effort here. Home now. Go on home! But the dog persisted and in truth he was glad of her company. It wasn't as if there was a lot of traffic to run her down. It must be a couple of miles to the main road where he might hope to get a lift, and surely she would give up on him long before he got there.

Best to go now, when the decision was made. No point hanging around. It wasn't that early for him. He had been getting up at five for the last thirty years. He was used to early starts. It was a habit he'd formed when he was first posted to India, to the plains where it was so hot and the early morning was the only time when it was cool. And the walk, even if he had to walk all the way, was only six miles or so, no distance, and on the flat. Like the plains, when he was a young man. Only, he wasn't used to the flat any more. He wasn't used to that, and he wasn't used to the lack of porters and to having to carry his own case, the handle that dug into his cold hands, which

223

would have been better off with gloves only he didn't have any. It disturbed him, the horizontal land, the straight lines of the roads and of the hedges beside them, the bare elms rearing up in the fog. Walking on the flat in this fog seemed an abstract activity, almost like walking on the spot, if it had not been for the changing forms of those elms, or a lone oak he passed, or a break of Scots pines. And for the dog, who still came with him.

Then he heard a car coming behind, turned and saw its lights yellowish in the fog. He stood on the verge, the case in one hand, the dog held back by her collar in the other.

The car stopped for him. Window wound down. A man in a brown tweed jacket, brown eyes, balding.

Can I give you a lift?

He reached across and opened the door.

Where are you going?

Swaffham?

I can take you to Swaffham. Don't worry about the dog, she'll find her way back. Won't you, Jess? Go on off home now.

You know her?

I'm the local doctor. I know everyone round here, and their dogs too. Nice young couple, the Ashes. She'll be due any time now. That'll be good to see.

The doctor drove, and didn't ask any questions. Perhaps there were others like him these days, on the road in the morning with their cases in their hands. How was he to know?

But where were you going? I don't want to take you out of your way.

The doctor gave a slight smile, shook his head. I was on a call. I was just going home, but I don't think I'm ready for home just yet. Driving's fine.

Perhaps he had been attending a death. That was what doctors did in the early hours. A death, or a birth. Somehow it didn't seem like it was a birth. He peered at the road ahead, his hands patient on the wheel. There was no hurry in the fog.

She managed a stretch of sleep for an hour before dawn, but woke and felt a cramp just as Hussey went downstairs. The floors and walls were thin in this old house. She heard him in the kitchen. She could have gone down herself, sleepy, hair askew, whale-shape wrapped in her pink dressing gown, and made him tea or breakfast or whatever he wanted – but no, she thought, that was what he didn't want. He was a lone man who wanted to be alone. Here he didn't fit. Let him be, she thought, let him go, hearing the bolts drawn on the back door. Let him creep out, and take the past with him, whatever it was that they talked about all night, some past which she did not understand and could not enter, of which she was both jealous and afraid as if it held some threat to her or the child. She felt another sharp cramp. She had been having such cramps on and off for days. She was told that they preceded contractions. They were her muscles, the baby, preparing themselves. She lay on her back in the bed and held her two hands now to her belly, and Charlie snored peacefully beside her. He must have slept and sweated it out now, the night's drink and whatever had been said. Let Hussey go, and there would be just the three of them in the house. Then she slept again, deeply.

Charlie was already in the kitchen when she came down. He had the Aga stoked and the kettle on for breakfast.

Hussey's gone.

I thought I heard something.

When?

Early, I thought I heard him go out.

He left this note. I came down and there was this note on the table, and Jess was outside, she must have gone out with him. Her coat was wet as if she'd been a long way.

Claire yawned and pulled a chair back and sat down, away from the table where she had space.

I had such a bad night. I kept waking up. She spoke in a tired vague voice. I think I heard him. I think I even knew he was going. I just didn't think I should stop him.

No, he said, but what he meant by the word wasn't clear.

You were up for ages, what did you talk about? I heard you laughing.

Did we laugh? I don't remember.

What'll he do?

Go to Kenya I suppose like he says in the note. Here, read it.

You were right, darling. Home's not his home, is it?

He picked up the note again from the table where she'd put it down. Odd thing, you know. I don't think I've ever once called him Jack.

The fog was slow to lift. The first moment some light broke through, Claire saw it and went out and picked daffodils to bring in to the house. Was it because she was so tired that the brightness of the flowers disturbed her? They stood up crude and yellow from the dull March ground, when everything about them seemed to have settled numbly back into winter. When she snapped the hollow stems the smell of them stung with its greenness. She arranged them indoors where they looked suddenly happier, and she built a fire in the sitting room and lit it, as though they still had a guest in the house. Or perhaps it was to draw Charlie into the room, so that they might sit a part of the day before the fire with the dog on the rug and the daffodils bright on the table before the window, an image of warmth and closeness that anyone outside would see should they come by and look in from the grey. That Hussey would see if he were to walk back, that would be too strong an image for him or any memory that he brought with him to break.

Charlie had spent much of the morning in his study.

What have you been doing?

Paperwork, he said.

I made a fire in the sitting room.

That's nice, he said, but went back to his study.

After lunch, it cleared. There was still no colour to the world apart from the daffs, but a milky distance at least. She thought that he should go out, work at something, do whatever it was that made a man feel sure of his place in the world. Turn thoughts to things.

Will you go out on the farm now?

It's been too wet, we still can't get on the land. Maybe tomorrow. Did you hear the forecast?

No. We'll have to make sure to listen later.

She thought she could not bear all that was unsaid. It hung about them like the day, whatever it was that he had talked about with Hussey. The war, the Japs, the Nagas, whatever it was that she didn't know. She had a sudden fear that he might all of a sudden take himself off, like Hussey, in the dawn when she slept or even in the day, in this not-broad daylight.

Sometime in the afternoon he came out from the study with his gun, called Jess to him, put on his coat and his boots and his cap. Said there would be pigeon for supper.

She smiled and spoke lightly. That was her part, to be light.

That'll be lovely, darling. The words floated and did not feel quite her own.

Come along, Jess.

He opened the door and the dog ran past and ahead of him across the yard. He had the gun under his arm. His boots sounded bright first on the cobbles and then more dully on the track. He opened a gate to a field, strode out across it, the golden dog running on, the mud gathering and weighing on his boots.

The field was ready to be drilled as soon as there was some warmth in the soil. The winter's plough was broken down, harrowed to a good smooth tilth. This field would be barley, this year. Claire was happy that they would have barley in the field in front of the house. It will be like having the sea before us, she had said. In June the purple tips of the crop would move like a sea, ruffled in the wind. And it would be gold, when it ripened, more golden than wheat. There was so much gold to come when now all was brown. The brown field, the brown spinney at the end of it, the ground of which was copper and brown with old sodden leaves. He took his position at the edge of the spinney, in his brown coat with his green-brown tweed cap, beside the trunk of an oak, hoping that his still form would merge in the pigeon's eye with the tree itself. Who knew what was in a pigeon's eye, the small black bead of it? A pigeon could identify movement a long way off. Pigeons were clever and watchful, even when they were flying home. But that was the moment to shoot them, nonetheless, when they were flying home at the end of the day, standing still as a tree, with the dog well trained beside you, still as yourself and the tree, standing within the home to which they were flying, where they would roost. So he stood and waited, very still, with the comforting weight of the gun in his hands. The dog waited beside him, but watching him and not the field. Only her tail moved, twitching on the brown leaves, and the breath from her open mouth. Good dog, Jess.

He flexed his fingers as they grew cold. He had listened to the forecast. The fog wasn't coming down again. The night would be clear and cold. The sky towards sunset was becoming unexpectedly lighter, pale turquoise-blue streaks bared in it, the first colour in all of that day. He saw the birds coming towards him, not a single one but half a dozen at once, and there would be more behind, but his first shot would serve to drive them all away, to wheel away and back and round, and gather again, and perhaps return when it was all the colder or find some other roost. He singled out one bird, shot, and it fell to the ground, and Jess ran for it and brought it back. He put the bird into his bag, moved along to another spot and began the wait again, alert, mind emptying of all but the sky as the brief light faded.

Grey dusk by the time he walked back, coming this time to the front of the house. Claire hadn't drawn the curtains yet. He could see into the sitting room, the fire still burning, that she had kept up all day; the mirror above the mantelpiece, the daffodils on the table before the window, the green armchairs and no one in them. But the front door was open, and Claire standing outside calling him. She was leaning against the doorframe, barefoot, feet flat to the stone of the doorstep, crying out and spreading her hands wide across the great curve of her belly – woman, just that, not Claire but woman – or no, just essentially Claire. In one smooth movement, he put the gun to the ground and ran towards her.